A Harvest Truce

Ukrainian Research Institute
Harvard University

Harvard Library of Ukrainian Literature 9

Cambridge, Massachusetts

SERHIY ZHADAN

A HARVEST TRUCE

A PLAY

Translated by
Nina Murray

50 years ■ 1973–2023

Distributed by Harvard University Press
for the Ukrainian Research Institute
Harvard University

The Harvard Ukrainian Research Institute was established in 1973 as an integral part of Harvard University. It supports research associates and visiting scholars who are engaged in projects concerned with all aspects of Ukrainian studies. The Institute also works in close cooperation with the Committee on Ukrainian Studies, which supervises and coordinates the teaching of Ukrainian history, language, and literature at Harvard University.

ISBN 9780674291997 (hardcover), 9780674292017 (paperback), 9780674292024 (epub), 9780674292031 (PDF)

Library of Congress Control Number: 2023942580
LC record available at https://lccn.loc.gov/2023942580

Cover image by Lesyk Panasiuk, https://www.gladunpanasiuk.com
Serhiy Zhadan's photo on the back of the cover by Anastasiia Mantach. Reproduced with permission
Book design by Andrii Kravchuk

Publication of this book has been made possible by the generous support of publications in Ukrainian studies at Harvard University by the following benefactors or funds endowed in their name:

Ostap and Ursula Balaban
Jaroslaw and Olha Duzey
Vladimir Jurkowsky
Myroslav and Irene Koltunik
Damian Korduba Family
Peter and Emily Kulyk
Irena Lubchak
Dr. Evhen Omelsky
Eugene and Nila Steckiw
Dr. Omeljan and Iryna Wolynec
Wasyl and Natalia Yerega

You can support our work of publishing academic books and translations of Ukrainian literature and documents by making a tax-deductible donation in any amount, or by including HURI in your estate planning.

To find out more, please visit https://huri.harvard.edu/give.

CONTENTS

MAIN CHARACTERS

Tolik Shevtsov
(also Anatoly,
Tolyan, Tolya,
Tokha, Tokh')

*A young man in his early thirties
of an unknown profession and
occupation*

Anton Shevtsov
(also Antosha,
Antosh',
Tosha, Tosh')

*Tolik's older brother from out of
town who runs a wholesale meat
business*

Aunt Shura

An older local woman

Katya and
Valichka (also
Valya, Val')

Aunt Shura's helpers

Kolya
(also Kolyan, Kol')

*A local farmer and neighbor of
the Shevtsovs*

Mashka
(also Masha,
Mash')

Kolya's pregnant wife

Rinat

The local mailman

To remember you, to come together and unfurl the scroll of memory, to pass what we know about you from one pair of hands to another, like a cup of water. To speak your name and remind ourselves that everything that has already happened is irreversible and what lies ahead is inevitable. The sound of your name wounds my voice, and my voice breaks like a reed in the hand of a child. What will become of us, those who have been granted the luxury of observing, the luxury of remembering, what are we to do with our past that turned out to be more powerful than our own will, louder, more potent? Our memories turn under the wind like sails, steer us to follow the sun, fill us with a bitter unease, make our hearts ache, tender as deep wounds suffered when we were children.

In our memory, homes light up in the dark, you can hear the river beyond the city, and the sky is a mosaic map of this world and all its secrets, all its nooks and crannies. In our memory, grass grows in the yards, the riverbank denudes itself after the long winter like living skin, and the voices that taught us to speak to trees and stones and birds, to every shadow and the smallest flame, draw nearer. Our memory could fill the chilled, abandoned apartments, it could heal an entire generation's despair, it could repair the fatigue of so many strong, grown people. We have enough memory to love you, but too little to bring you back.

It feels empty now without you, and the place where you had been, where I could hear your voice, has filled with the wind like a house left in a panic, a home where there's still a trace of the children's warmth and a woman's breath, a home that still retains a shadow of the solace it had been. The house where you had felt so happy, that you had tended and called your own, the house that had lost its song without you like a violin left in the bitter February cold.

I

A two-story house. A modest place, last renovated about ten years ago, with little furniture. The owners, it is obvious, had never been well-off and now times are really tough.

On the first floor, on the left is a refrigerator, and next to it a shower without a door, and a wardrobe. On the right is a couch. There is a large table in the middle of the room and a rug on the floor. On the second floor, to the left is a bedroom, door closed, and to the right an alcove with a bed in it.

TOLIK is sitting at the table. He is just over thirty, barefoot, and wearing a pair of long shorts and a Hawaiian shirt. He is eating breakfast cereal from a bowl.

ANTON, his older brother, enters. Anton is wearing jeans, a white shirt, and a sport coat. He is carrying a briefcase.

Anton looks nervous. Tolik, by contrast, is calm. Tolik looks up from his bowl.

TOLIK
What's up?

ANTON

The bridge is gone.

TOLIK

Been gone for a while. Got blown up a week ago.
Before the truce.

ANTON

I didn't know that.

TOLIK

Come home more often, dude.

ANTON
(*nervously*)

Home? When was the last time *you* called me?

TOLIK

What would I call you for? What are you, a
directory?

ANTON

Fuck, Tolya. The bridge is gone.

TOLIK

Sure is.

ANTON

I left my car back there, at the checkpoint on the
other side.

TOLIK

That was dumb.

ANTON

Speak for yourself. They just said, okay, dude, leave the car at the checkpoint and swim across.

TOLIK

You can forget about your car now.

ANTON

What do you mean, forget it? They'll give it back. We'll figure it out.

TOLIK

Uh-huh.

ANTON

What? You think they won't?

TOLIK

Right, they'll give it back and fill it up for you, too. At least they weren't shooting.

ANTON

How long has it been quiet?

TOLIK

Since Monday. It's the truce. The harvest one.

ANTON

(*distractedly*)

Oh yeah, right. The harvest one. They got me across in a rubber boat. There's no way to get here from downtown now. And it was such a nice road, everyone pitched in. And the bridge.

The Metropolitan himself came to open it, blessed it. They ruined it now. And took my jeep. Where is she?

TOLIK
(*continuing to eat*)
   Upstairs.

ANTON
   Why upstairs?

TOLIK
   What else am I supposed to do? Seat her at the table?

Anton starts to say something but stops himself. He goes to the fridge, looks inside it.

ANTON
   You got food?

TOLIK
   I've got beer.

ANTON
   Oh.

(*He pulls out a bottle of beer.*)

   It's warm!

TOLIK
   The fridge is off, dude. No power. All busted.

ANTON
Why'd you put the beer in there, then?

TOLIK
What, you don't put your beer in the fridge?

ANTON
I do.

TOLIK
Dude!

Anton controls himself, says nothing, comes back to the table, opens the beer, drinks for a long time, finally puts the bottle on the table. He opens his briefcase and pulls out cans of food.

ANTON
Here, open one. You eat like a student.

TOLIK
Thanks, bro.

Anton puts the cans on the table, steps up to Tolik, hesitates, silent, for a moment, then hugs Tolik's head in his arms and presses him against his chest in an awkward hug. Anton starts to cry.

ANTON
It's okay, brother. It's okay. We'll figure it out. It's okay.

Tolik says nothing. Anton, relieved by crying, wipes his tears with one arm, while holding the other around Tolik's neck.

ANTON
How are you doing?

TOLIK
(*strangled*)
I can't breathe.

ANTON
I understand. I've got this lump in my throat, too—right here.

TOLIK
Let go of my neck. You're choking me.

Anton lets go, straightens his sport coat, embarrassed.

ANTON
So, what now, bro? What are we going to do?

Tolik shrugs. Anton gets up, picks up the cans from the table, goes to the fridge and puts the cans inside. He pulls out another beer. He goes to sit back at the table, takes a mouthful of Tolik's cereal, washes it down with beer.

ANTON
I'll go up. I have to.

TOLIK
Leave the beer.

Anton leaves the beer and climbs the stairs to the second floor where he steps over various kitchen objects strewn all over the floor. He comes to the closed door. Stands there, collecting himself. Finally, he opens the door decisively, goes into the room, and closes the door behind him. A few seconds later he falls backward out of the room, closes the door, and silently comes downstairs. He picks up his beer and finishes it.

ANTON
You should at least tidy up there. It's a mess.

TOLIK
Right, I've been waiting for you to tell me.
I just sat there thinking, when Anton Petrovych comes, he'll tell me what to do.

ANTON
Alright, alright, don't start. What are we going to do?

TOLIK
Well, I thought you would come, we'd load your car, and go.

ANTON
Load what? There's no bridge! Can't drive here.

TOLIK
I'm aware.

ANTON
So now what?

TOLIK

> Guess we should call downtown, the
> administration, let them figure it out.

ANTON

> Could we do it ourselves?

TOLIK

> Carry her all the way downtown? It's six miles.
> And no bridge. You gonna ford that river?

ANTON

> Could we go around? How far is it to the next
> bridge?

TOLIK

> There are checkpoints there, too. And not
> clear whose. I'd say it's eighteen miles, as the
> crow flies.

ANTON

> Whoa... Who do you know in the administration?

TOLIK

> Sanya.

ANTON

> Who's that?

TOLIK

> The mayor.

ANTON

Sanya is the mayor? I thought he was doing time.

TOLIK

He might be now. Saw him on TV a week ago.
Before the power went.

ANTON

What did he say?

TOLIK

He said he was for peace. That there would be a
truce. The harvest one. So I guess he's not in jail
at the moment.

ANTON

Do you have his number?

TOLIK

(*pulls out an old Nokia*)
But you call him. I won't.

ANTON

Why not?

TOLIK

Well, I'm, like, the opposition.

ANTON

The what?

TOLIK

I owe him money, that's what.

ANTON
(*annoyed*)
> Damn it. (*He looks through the contacts on the phone.*) You don't have any Mayor Sanya here.

TOLIK
> Look under ZH.

ANTON
> Why ZH?

TOLIK
> He's Zhora.

ANTON
> Why Zhora?

TOLIK
> That's what people call him. Zhora. Zhora the mayor.

Anton dials.

ANTON
> The signal's shit.

TOLIK
> You got it. It's shit down here. You have to go upstairs. But don't take too long—the battery runs down.

Anton, irritated, runs upstairs. Dials.

ANTON
(*shouts to Tolik, downstairs*)
　　No signal here either.

TOLIK
　　Get on a chair!

ANTON
　　What?

TOLIK
　　Get your ass on a chair!

Anton grabs a chair, climbs onto it, dials again.

ANTON
(*when the call connects*)
　　Hello! Zhora? Sanya? Sasha? Sasha, hi. This is
　　Anton. Shevtsov. That's right, himself. Thank
　　you, yeah, me too. Sasha, we've got a situation
　　here. Mom died. Yes, our mom. The legal one.
　　Yep, completely. Yes, thank you, thank you...
　　We're sorry too. The problem? The problem is
　　there is no bridge. Yeah, I know you know, sure.
　　We live on the other side, by the old base. So
　　what should we do? We can't get her across on
　　pontoons, right? And we can't just leave her here
　　either, gotta bury her properly, with paperwork
　　and all, right? Right. So I thought you, as the
　　authorities, might help us out? What? What
　　she's doing? What is she doing—she's dead, like I
　　said. She just lies there. Where? What difference
　　does that make? She's fine. Dead, but fine. We

have to bury her, it's summer... Yeah? You will?
When? Tomorrow? For sure? Yes, we'll get the
papers. Thank you, Zhora. Sanya, Sasha. Thank
you, yes, we'll wait, of course. Thank you, sure.
Of course—we're businessmen, we'll figure it out.
Where I'm calling from? (*Anton looks around him,
grabs a towel that's hanging off the chandelier.*)
From my office. Right. Aha. Thank you!

He gets off the chair and comes downstairs.

ANTON

It's fine. He can't do it today, he's got OSCE
there. He said he'll figure something out
tomorrow.

TOLIK

What is he going to figure out? Send a canoe?

ANTON

He'll think of something. He's the mayor, people
elected him.

TOLIK

Uh-huh.

ANTON

Don't worry, bro. We'll figure it out. Family is
sacred.

TOLIK

You sounded just like our old man there. You actually remind me of him a lot. At your worst, I mean.

ANTON

Like he was ever anything else. Although... He did like to sing.

TOLIK

Dude, he only sang when he was drunk or...

ANTON

Or what?

TOLIK

Or he didn't.

Anton sits quietly for a bit, then can't stand it anymore, jumps to his feet, goes to the fridge and gets out two more beers. He opens both, hands one to Tolik and drinks the other one himself.

TOLIK

It's warm.

ANTON

Yep. Warm, damn it.

They drink more.

ANTON

Hey. How long has she been there like that?

TOLIK

Bro, I don't know.

ANTON

What do you mean you don't know? When was the last time you two talked?

TOLIK

We didn't.

ANTON

What do you mean you didn't?

TOLIK

The fuck do you want from me? We weren't talking, okay? We were mad at each other.

ANTON

How so?

TOLIK

Well, she was hard to talk to, okay? She'd watch TV all morning and then start raving.

ANTON

And what did you do?

TOLIK

Watched TV with her. What else is there to do here? When the shooting started, we just stayed in and watched TV. No work anywhere. Plenty of war, but no work. And then, at the end, there was no power, so no TV either. We just stayed in our corners, not speaking to each other. I wouldn't have known something was wrong with her. Found her in the morning when I went in to ask where her glasses were.

ANTON

Her glasses.

TOLIK

I wear them to read.

ANTON

You wear her glasses to read?

TOLIK

Tokha, what are you confused about? That I wear her glasses to read or that I read things, period? Were you not aware that I can read?

ANTON

Alright, alright.

TOLIK

No, not alright. Basically, I went in, and she was there. Done. So I climbed onto the chair and called you.

ANTON

I'm glad you did. Here's what I'm thinking: I'm thinking we should clean up this place.

TOLIK

Go ahead, knock yourself out.

ANTON
> Oh, come on! People from the administration are coming. From Zhora, tomorrow.

TOLIK
> You mean from Sasha.

ANTON
> Right. Zhora. Sasha. They'll come take her away. We'll have a wake.

TOLIK
> With warm beer.

ANTON
> Don't get hung up on the beer. With something else. Either way, we have to clean up. Can't have people here with the place looking like this. We are a family.

TOLIK
> What people, bro? There isn't anyone around. When the shooting started, everyone left.

ANTON
(*serious now*)
> She would have been happy to know that we tidied up. She liked to have things in order.

TOLIK
> She sure did. I could never find anything. She hid everything.

ANTON

She liked to pick things up.

TOLIK

Yep, like a magpie. You couldn't leave anything lying around—she'd snatch it.

ANTON

Exactly. I always thought she was like a magpie, too.

TOLIK

You did?

ANTON

Sure. She used to make so much noise. Like a magpie.

TOLIK

She sure did. Remember that time she lost you on the beach? When we were still kids?

ANTON

I do. You were drunk, too.

TOLIK

I sure was. So were you, by the way. I just fell asleep by her side and stayed put. I didn't get lost. But you did.

ANTON

I was a kid, remember?

TOLIK

A kid who should of drunk less, bro. You managed to get lost on the Azov Sea.

ANTON

And later, remember, the three of us sat on the beach all night, and she kept singing.

TOLIK

Yeah. That was horrible.

ANTON

You said it.

TOLIK

The old man was not there.

ANTON

He was never there.

TOLIK

Thank God. Else, he, too, would have wanted to sing.

Both fall silent.

TOLIK

Alright, fuck it. Let's clean up here. It would make her happy.

ANTON

That's the spirit! You go ahead, I'm gonna jump
into the shower. I'll just be a minute, and we'll
get it all done. I'll take care of it.

*Anton heads for the shower stall. Tolik, at the same time,
gets up, looks around the room and notices the rug on
the floor. Anton takes off his clothes, down to his boxer
shorts. Tolik, meanwhile, rolls up the rug and drags it to
the front of the stage.*

ANTON
(*loudly*)

That's right, Tokha, we'll take care of everything.
It will be fine. You did good to call me right
away. If only you hadn't fought with mom...
But, then again, she was a piece of work herself.
I should know, I remember it. The main thing for
you now, bro, is to stay calm. Zhora, Sasha—the
mayor—he'll drop by tomorrow and we'll get it
all done. Okay, then, here we go!

*Turns the faucet decisively, with his face turned up to
catch the water. There is no water. Tolik sits down on
the rolled-up rug and lights a cigarette. Anton turns the
faucet furiously. There is no water.*

ANTON

Tokha! There's no water.

TOLIK

That's right. No water, either.

ANTON

What am I supposed to do?

TOLIK

I could douse you with beer, if you'd like.

Anton, irritated, puts his boxers and t-shirt back on and runs back into the kitchen. He sees Tolik there.

ANTON

What is this?

TOLIK

The rug. It came from India. Mom's dowry.

ANTON

I mean, what is this? You smoke? Does Mom even know?

TOLIK

I don't have a mom, dude. I'm an orphan now. And so are you, by the way.

Anton stands still as if remembering something, then sits down next to Tolik, hugs him, and begins to cry again. Tolik is tense and silent and does not try to shake his brother off.

ANTON

That's just the story of my life, you know? Just miserable. No luck whatsoever. Back since high school. I know, things were tough for you here. Back when, you know, all this started.

TOLIK

Yeah, I got it.

ANTON

I don't want to say it out loud, but you know?

TOLIK

I said I got it.

ANTON

I know it's hard for you to talk about this.

TOLIK

Alright already.

ANTON

Okay, okay, I won't. Anyway, I was still in high school when I knew something was wrong. Like I was cursed, you know? Marked. A lone wolf, like. Our parents loved me less, too. Don't even—I know I'm right. Do you think I couldn't see it? They couldn't get enough of you. I could see it all. I told myself then: no one is going to protect you. You gonna have to take care of yourself. So I did. I barely even saw the old man, and Mom was all about you. I was still in school when I started my first business. Started to bring money home.

TOLIK

I thought you stole it from someone else.

ANTON

> That's not the point. I went to the university
> then—got in on my own, without any help from
> our parents. You know what that means? And
> I kept working. I've been working all my life.
> I knew no one had my back. I had to take care
> of myself. I'm a self-made man, Tokha, get it?
> Don't think I'm complaining or anything... Not at
> all. I made my own choices. I worked and I told
> myself: I can do it, I will get out of here. I'll make
> so much money I'll never have to come back,
> come home. Never have to cross that fucking
> bridge again. I'll have a nice house, a nice job, I'll
> have a family, everything. I just had to take care
> of myself. Depend on no one. Trust nobody. I'm a
> lone wolf, you know? A wolf!

TOLIK

> Dude!

ANTON

(*not listening to him*)

> Do you know when it all changed? At the
> university. I finally found a good client. I helped
> him with something, he sent something my way.
> And then he put in a word for me at a pretty
> serious firm. Give it a shot, he told me. It might
> not work. I don't know if you'll fit in there—or
> if you'll survive. Not everyone can stand it, he
> said, the business breaks people.

TOLIK

> Sure. Like Baikonur. Cosmonaut camp.

ANTON

Fuck off. So there I was—I came to their office, put on a suit and all. The first suit I ever had, Tokha, bought it from another guy, second-hand, but it was a good brand, you know? I'm thinking, I can do it, I'll fit in, this is my chance. I'll figure it all out. So I go in to see the boss—Ivan Ivanovych, I remember his name. He's there in his chair, and, like, dying.

TOLIK

Why?

ANTON

Diabetes.

TOLIK

So what?

ANTON

Well, he drank a lot, too.

TOLIK

Ah. Our old man had diabetes too.

ANTON

Anyway, there he sits, and you can see him decomposing right in front of you. He smells like a corpse. Kind of like Mom smells right now...

(He starts crying again.)

Oh, brother.

TOLIK
(*comforts him*)
Alright now, come on.

ANTON
Okay, okay, I'm alright, I'm good. Sorry. So, yeah. There he sits and stares at me, and I'm what, a boy basically, and I'm looking at him and wondering, what am I going to say? He's basically a cadaver, he looks like the meat he sells. But he's the boss, and I'm a dick from Cunthill. Metaphorically speaking.

TOLIK
I got you.

ANTON
He says to me: you won't cut it in our business, son, no way. You are too nice. Man can't be nice in our business, that's not the kind of work we do. You have to have a heart of iron. Men here tear each other's throats out with their teeth. There's no thinking of anyone else in our trade. You've got to fight for every bite. Like a wolf. Break bones, snap tendons.

TOLIK
Are you sure he had diabetes?

ANTON
So, he says, you better not even try. And looks at me, sizes me up. And I'm standing there and you know what I'm thinking? I'm thinking of our

old man. Seriously. How he'd stumble home, sit here, at this table, and just stay there, for days. Never went anywhere. Just sat and never spoke a word. If I asked him something, he never answered. Just sat there, like a zombie, and never spoke. So I'm looking at that Ivan fucking Ivanovych, and thinking, I'm gonna outlive you, bitch, you can bet on that. Just to fuck you all. Stab me, cut me, break my bones—I'll outlive you. I'll be sitting at that desk of yours and fucking with you all. Kind of like you are, right now. That's alright, Ivan Ivanovych, I said. I want to give it a shot, I'm sure of it. He went all tense, but then said, okay then, be my guest. So I gave it a shot. And I was good at it. You know what I mean? I did it. All by myself. I'm a self-made man.

TOLIK
Spiderman.

ANTON
Well... C'mon, Tokh', don't be mad at me. I don't mean it like that. I've always loved you, you know that. Remember that time you fell into the lake and I pulled you out? Mom yelled at both of us. Remember?

TOLIK
"Fell in"? You were the one who shoved me. Why would I have fallen?

ANTON
(*bitter*)
> Yeah? So you do remember. If your memory's so good, why don't you tell me what to do about the paperwork. What's she's got left? Her passport?

TOLIK
> The passport's definitely here somewhere.

ANTON
> Wouldn't hurt to find it. We'll need it for the paperwork. Where did she keep it? The house deed? The land?

TOLIK
> Oh, the deeds. She hid it all, put it all away—your guess is as good as mine. Before she died, I know for sure she went over everything. Like she knew what was coming. Right... Right! The briefcase. Remember the briefcase I had? That's where she put everything.

ANTON
> So where is it, this briefcase?

TOLIK
> Fuck if I know.

ANTON
> They won't take her without the papers.

TOLIK

Nah—it's not like they'd just leave her here.

ANTON

Like hell they won't. There's a war on, haven't you heard?

TOLIK

Alright, alright. What's wrong with you?

ANTON

Oh, you don't know? That's right, you've got no TV and the mail doesn't come here. Does anything come into that thick skull of yours? I've got it all worked out, they'll come get her tomorrow, from downtown, over that fucking bridge.

TOLIK

Why are you shouting?

ANTON

Why? Because I've worked everything out, I've called that fucking mayor, I've taken care of it all. And they'll come tomorrow, somehow, and then what? Hi, where's your Mrs. Shevtsov, right? And I'm like: Hi, here she is, been like that three days already, waiting for you. Rotting like a pumpkin.

TOLIK

Alright, come on now.

ANTON
And they're like: okay, do you have her passport?
Any ID?

TOLIK
Dude, don't get worked up now, okay? What
would they want her passport for? They are not
selling her alcohol.

ANTON
They'll be selling alcohol to you, dumb-ass! Her,
they have to bury. With honors. As a veteran
of labor. Just as long as you can show them her
passport and prove you didn't fish her out of the
river after the last rains.

TOLIK
What rains, dude? Summer's been dry, wheat's
like tinder.

ANTON
(*faces Tolik, in an icy tone*)
Where are her papers?

TOLIK
Fuck if I know.

ANTON
(*moves in closer*)
Where are the papers?

TOLIK
Dude. Don't start.

ANTON
    The papers?

TOLIK
    Fuck you!

Anton hits Tolik suddenly on the back of his head. Tolik falls down onto the table, then jumps back up and lunges at Anton. Anton hist him again. Tolik falls onto the table again. He jumps up, dashes past Anton onto the couch and flings himself onto it, face down. He grabs his head with his hands and weeps desperately.

Anton, still breathing hard, goes to the fridge and pulls out a beer. He turns, looks at his brother, and pulls out a second beer. He takes the beers to the table, opens both bottles, and takes a long, greedy drink from his. He sits silently for some time, listening to his brother's weeping. Finally, he can't stand it anymore.

ANTON
    Okay now, alright. Come on.

Tolik goes on weeping.

ANTON
    Come on, bro. Come on already.

He goes to the couch with a bottle of beer.

ANTON
    Here, have a drink. Go ahead, drink some.

Anton turns around and returns to the table. Tolik, not looking up at Anton, holds out his hand. Anton hands him the bottle, and Tolik takes a drink from it, still not getting up. He hands the bottle back to Anton and starts sobbing again.

Anton sits down next to him on the couch.

ANTON

Alright, Tolya, alright. Come on, now. I'm sorry, I just lost it. It's the stress, on my feet all day, and the car got taken. It's like you said, the fuckers won't give it back, right? I'm sorry. It's because of Mom.

Tolik pulls himself up and sits next to Anton. He is speaking through sobs.

TOLIK

Oh yeah? Because of Mom? Like I'm not... about Mom. Like I'm mad about the weather or something. Like, you're the good son, right, and I'm the kind that carries off radiators for scrap? You think I don't miss her? I don't even have anyone, except her. The old man's gone, you are at your slaughterhouse, with your cadavers...

ANTON

Carcasses.

TOLIK

What?

ANTON
> Carcasses. That's what I sell. Oh fuck, it's all
> gonna go to hell in this heat... While I'm sitting
> here with you, dealing with the family stuff.

TOLIK
> Fine, carcasses. D'you think it makes me happy
> to have her lying there, starting to rot? You
> all disappeared when this shit started. You
> think she didn't ask about you? As soon as the
> shooting started, the first thing: Where's Anton?
> Like I'm not even there. She didn't even know me
> at the end. I'd take her food and she wouldn't
> open the door. How'd you think that felt, huh?
> D'you think I didn't want to fuck off from here?
> Think I didn't know they'd blow up that bridge,
> didn't see the way things were going? You
> downtown types scheme your schemes, and shit
> goes "boom" over here.

*Anton wraps his arms around Tolik's neck. They cry
together. There's a text message alert.*

ANTON
(not letting go of Tolik, pulls out his phone, checks it)
> Hey, a text came through. It's from work. I'll
> just write back.

*Leaves Tolik's side, goes upstairs and climbs on the chair.
Starts typing a message.*

ANTON
> Sorry, bro. It's from work.

TOLIK

Yeah, and who cares about me? You've got work,
you've got your business, your slaughterhouse.
And what about me?

ANTON

I'll just be a second, Tolya.

TOLIK

So I'm stuck here with our crazy mom, and he's
a lone wolf.

ANTON

Much health and happiness...

TOLIK

What?

ANTON

Much health and happiness. That's what I'm
saying.

TOLIK

What are you doing right now?

ANTON

Sending birthday greetings.

TOLIK

To whom?

ANTON

Our accountant.

TOLIK
Are you serious?

ANTON
Yeah, why?

TOLIK
Are you kidding me? I'm sitting here spilling
my guts before this guy, and he's texting his
accountant. You better send a selfie, too. In your
underpants. To your accountant. I bet you send
each other pictures like that all the time.

ANTON
Like what?

TOLIK
Underpant selfies.

ANTON
Tolya, my accountant is a very serious, married
man. Why would I want his selfie?

TOLIK
Never mind. Happiness and health. You want me
to find you something to wear around here?

ANTON
(*as he finishes typing*)
...and health. Right. Send. Yes, please.

*Tolik stands up and lifts the seat of the folding couch.
From the storage space inside, he pulls out a pair of*

sweatpants and a sweater, then a black briefcase. He picks up the briefcase and puts it on the table.

TOLIK
The briefcase.

ANTON
(still on the chair)
What's that?

TOLIK
The briefcase. The one with the papers.

Anton jumps down from the chair and runs down the stairs. The two brothers lean over the briefcase.

ANTON
Where was it?

TOLIK
Inside the couch.

ANTON
Open it.

Tolik clicks the briefcase open and pulls out a piece of paper.

TOLIK
Utility bills. And here's the deed to the house. And my birth certificate.

ANTON

An album. Photos.

TOLIK

Right, look, that's her. She was cute, right?

ANTON

What's with the peasants? Whose lap is she sitting on?

TOLIK

Those are her parents, dude. She's, like, four.

ANTON

What parents?

TOLIK

The ones she had: Grandma Lyusya and Grandpa.

ANTON

For real? So weird—must be the angle.

TOLIK

And here, look, that's you. With your arm in a cast, see?

ANTON

Oh yeah, I was into sports then.

TOLIK

You fell out the window, dude. Did you forget? And here's me, next to you. I look funny here, right?

ANTON
You look like shit.

TOLIK
That's what I mean. Look, I'm holding dad's service cap.

ANTON
Uh-huh. I remember it. Dad used to lose it all the time, the neighbors would bring it back.

TOLIK
A military man can't be without his cap.

ANTON
And here, look: that's when we just came back from GDR, right after we moved in here. The lady upstairs was still alive.

TOLIK
Right. She died pretty soon, though.

ANTON
Didn't take much with us around.

TOLIK
Oh, look at my cool cowboy outfit! The old man bought it in Leipzig. I remember I wore it to school, and the kids beat me up on the spot.

ANTON
Aha. I stood up for you then.

TOLIK

Yep. They beat you up, too.

ANTON

I don't remember that.

TOLIK

And here, look: that's when Mom's brother came to visit, Uncle Sam. From Donetsk. With his kids. Remember them? They just kept staring.

ANTON

I do. For whatever reason, Mom loved them.

TOLIK

She did. She used to call them. Both kids are fighting now.

Both are silent for a moment.

ANTON

They didn't come here though, did they?

TOLIK

Who?

ANTON

These—the relatives.

TOLIK

I don't think so.

ANTON

Mom called them from your cell?

TOLIK

She did. Why?

ANTON

Delete their numbers.

TOLIK

You think?

ANTON

I do.

The brothers are silent for a while as they focus on sorting through the documents.

ANTON

What's this notebook?

TOLIK

It's mine.

ANTON

What's in it?

TOLIK

Doesn't matter.

ANTON

No, wait. Did you write this?

TOLIK
Give it to me!

(He snatches the notebook out of Anton's hand and puts it away in the briefcase.)

ANTON
What's it about?

TOLIK
The weather. Moving on.

ANTON
Whatever.

They keep sorting through the papers.

ANTON
Okay, here's her tax ID, and her retirement certificate. Did you find her passport?

TOLIK
There is no passport.

ANTON
Where could it possibly be? Could she have left it somewhere? Like, did she go to the post office?

TOLIK
The post office is closed, why would she go there?

ANTON
Utilities company?

TOLIK
Don't be an idiot.

ANTON
Where is it then?

TOLIK
She went to vote.

ANTON
What?

TOLIK
She voted. Went to vote.

ANTON
When?

TOLIK
Just now. Couple months ago.

ANTON
What did she wear?

TOLIK
Like I remember? Her jacket.

ANTON
Where is it? C'mon!

The brothers close the lid of the briefcase and rush to the wardrobe. They put the briefcase inside and start tossing

pieces of clothing off the hangers. They find cardigans,
coats, and a fur coat.

ANTON
  Look in the pockets.

Tolik grabs the fur coat and carries it to the front of the
stage. He searches the pockets, feels deep inside the sleeves,
gets agitated, turns the coat inside out, loses his balance, falls
on the floor and tears at the fur as if it were a wild beast.
  Anton stops whatever he is doing, comes and looks at
his brother. Tolik continues wrestling with the fur coat on
the floor.

ANTON
  You okay?

TOLIK
(*angrily trying to free his arm from a sleeve*)
  Fucking bitch...

ANTON
  Bro, hey, are you okay?

TOLIK
  You fucking bitch...

ANTON
  Bro!

Anton gets a hold of the fur coat and pulls it toward
himself. Tolik resists, but Anton wins. He takes the fur
coat and checks the inside pocket.

ANTON
Got it.

TOLIK
You got it?

ANTON
Sure did. There's something here.

Anton produces a wad of cash. Tolik gets up from the floor, comes closer.

ANTON
What is this?

TOLIK
Her stash. (*Takes the money from Anton and weighs the wad on his hand.*) Mom saved up for her funeral.

ANTON
It's Soviet money.

TOLIK
She saved it in advance.

ANTON
I wish she'd spent it on a vacation. Even just once. Alright. We'll put it in the grave with her, let her have a good time in the land of the dead. The passport, though. Where is her passport?

Returns to the wardrobe and continues emptying it. Tolik puts the money on the table, then goes to Anton and tries to stop him.

ANTON
    The bedding. In the sheets. Of course!

Reaches deep inside the wardrobe and pulls out a long object. Unwraps it. It's a sniper rifle. Anton, lost, looks at Tolik—he clearly doesn't know what to say. A pause.

TOLIK
(in a quiet, cold voice)
    Give it here.

He steps closer and tries to take the rifle from Anton. Anton does not let go. The two stand in silence in the middle of the room. There's a knock on the door. The brothers quickly hide the rifle inside the couch. They stand there silent, waiting, afraid.

II

We were blessed with the feeling of safety in this house. The feeling of quiet on the hillsides, the coolness in the wells. We were blessed with the feeling of warmth in the morning and coolness in the evenings. So much light streamed each morning through our windows. So much moisture beaded on the branches of the cherry tree. We lived acutely aware of being given all this to see, to be a part of, of being given the sense that nothing happened without us.

Everything that mattered was given to us with the understanding that you would share the joy of being in this world as well, of finding these shores. Everything that hurt was sent to us so we could earn the right to be with you. We were given things only so that we could share them, so that we could see them only in your presence—when your shadow fell across this threshold, when your voice echoed from the street in the evening.

The gold of the late-summer greenery, the swelling of silence at the end of a long hot day—and you walking lightly across the field, your return to this home where you were so missed, where life without you stopped and lost all odds of regularity. Ghostly shapes will come for you—they will remind us about you, will try to summon you, will speak of you. How could I fill this void in my language where you used to be? How can I fill the silence left once I could no longer call out your name? Grow, my silence, grow bigger, heavier. Find your revelation. Let women's hands make all the choices; let women's voices tell everything there is to tell—who could ever stop them, who could understand them? Who?

Enter three women dressed in black. They stand in the middle of the room and look at the two men in silence. The first woman is AUNT SHURA: she is the eldest and speaks for all three. The second woman, KATIA, and the third woman, VALICHKA, stand behind her.

AUNT SHURA
How are you?

ANTON
Aunt Shura?

AUNT SHURA
Anton? You came back, then?

ANTON
I did.

AUNT SHURA
Why are you in your underpants?

ANTON
I went into the shower.

AUNT SHURA (*suspiciously*)
You have water?

TOLIK
Nope.

AUNT SHURA
(*turns to the other women, loudly*)
No water here either!

The women nod sympathetically.

AUNT SHURA
The pipe's been hit. Three days since. And there's no power. Nothing.

Everyone is silent.

ANTON
So, yeah, Aunt Shura, that's how things are.

AUNT SHURA
I know. That's why we came.

ANTON
You do?

AUNT SHURA
I do. Where is she?

TOLIK
Upstairs.

AUNT SHURA (*turns around, loudly*)
Let's go! Follow me!

TOLIK
Where are you going?

AUNT SHURA
She needs to be washed.

TOLIK
(*unhappy*)
What for? She's clean.

AUNT SHURA
Tolya, how about you let me decide who needs to be washed and who doesn't?

TOLIK
This is actually my house, Aunt Shura.

AUNT SHURA
Sure it is. Are you going to wash her?

TOLIK
Why are you all hung up on this washing thing?

(*He turns to Anton.*)

What's that for?

ANTON
I don't know. Hygiene, maybe.

AUNT SHURA
Hygiene is when you brush your teeth. The deceased must be washed because that's the order of things. The rule, do you understand? Or do you not understand?

ANTON
Okay, alright, fine, Aunt Shura. What are you going to wash her with?

The second woman comes to the table and pulls out two-liter bottles of water from her grocery bag. She puts them on the table.

ANTON
(*suspiciously*)
Is that mineral water?

AUNT SHURA
What else?

TOLIK
Sparkling?

ANTON
Is that allowed?

AUNT SHURA
It is. For the sick, those in the middle of a journey, and those who are pregnant.

ANTON
Well, sure. The pregnant ones.

AUNT SHURA
Shame we can't have a priest. But that's okay,
I'll manage. I know how.

ANTON
We'll manage. What happened to the priest?

AUNT SHURA
He's off fighting. Two months since.

ANTON
For which side?

AUNT SHURA
For the Christian faith.

(*She turns to one of the women.*)

Come on!

TOLIK
Frigging Crusaders...

*Aunt Shura climbs the stairs to the second floor. The
second woman grabs the water bottles and hurries
after her.*

AUNT SHURA
(*from upstairs, to the third woman, loudly*)
Valichka, tidy up there! People will come.

The third woman looks around the room and starts toward the couch.

ANTON
　　Hey!

Valichka does not hear him. She makes to unfold the couch flat.

TOLIK
　　Hello!

Valichka still does not hear them. Tolik runs up to her, grabs her hand. The woman looks at him, surprised.

TOLIK
　　What'd you think you're doing?

ANTON
　　She must be deaf.

TOLIK
(*looks back at him*)
　　What?

ANTON
　　She's deaf.

TOLIK
　　What do you mean, deaf?

ANTON
> Deaf as a doorknob. Can't you see? You know that dorm for the deaf, downtown?

TOLIK
> So?

ANTON
> That's where Aunt Shura gets them.

TOLIK
> How's she gonna clean if she's deaf?

(*He turns back to Valichka, speaks loudly.*)

> What are you going to clean?

Valichka looks back at him, says nothing.

TOLIK
> What are you, deaf?

ANTON
> Let her go. She's probably mute, too.

Tolik looks at Valichka, then lets go of her hand with distrust in his eyes.

TOLIK
(*loudly, to Valichka*)
> Don't clean here, you get it? Go over there.

Valichka, irked, goes back to the wardrobe. She opens it and starts tossing things out into one giant pile in the middle of the rug. Tolik looks like he's about to say something, but Anton hugs him and the two sit down on the couch.

TOLIK
(glances at Valichka)
> You think she's really deaf?

ANTON
> Sure. Deaf as a post. Can't you tell just by looking at her?

TOLIK
> How could you tell by looking?

ANTON
> You know. Look at her brow ridge.

TOLIK
> At her what?

ANTON
> Her brow ridge. I was into physiognomy, once.

TOLIK
> And?

ANTON
> With the kind of physiognomies we have around here, it doesn't help. Why are you all worked up?

TOLIK

I, dude, am worked up for one simple reason:
a decent search of this place could turn up
enough to get us ten years in the slammer.

ANTON

Sure. If not fifteen. Where'd you get that rifle?

TOLIK

Doesn't matter.

ANTON

Is that why you're afraid?

TOLIK

I'm not afraid.

ANTON

Sure. Then what did that woman do to you?
She's just a woman—cute, in a way. And deaf.

TOLIK

Right. With her brows. And the ridge thereof.

*Tolik nervously glances at Valichka who is now digging
through the pile of clothing, then whispers to Anton.*

TOLIK

Bro, what'd they come here for?

ANTON

What do you mean?

TOLIK
Did you call them?

ANTON
I take it, they are the community.

TOLIK
Right, the clean-up crew. They just go around washing corpses.

ANTON
You know. They are forward-thinking. With their mineral water.

TOLIK
Tokha, I'm serious. They'll rat us out. You'll see. Aunt Shura is a whole separate thing. She's the priest here, and the mayor. The secular and spiritual authority in a single person, so to speak. Washing the dead. She goes around to sniff out who's on whose side. She'll rat us out.

ANTON
To whom?

TOLIK
The highest bidder. They'll turn this place upside down, find our stuff, and that's it—we're as good as dead.

ANTON
Oh, come on!

TOLIK

What, you think they'll just let it slide? Like
they'll find what we have here and let us go? I'm
telling you, they've been sent here.

(*He turns to the woman.*)

Hey! You!

The woman does not look up and keeps doing her work.

TOLIK

How do you think they found out? About
Mom, like?

ANTON
(*loud and confident*)

Sasha must have told them. I mean, Zhora. They
elected him mayor, didn't they? So he told them.

TOLIK

Right. And then he air-dropped them here, right?
His deaf paratroopers brigade.

ANTON

Come on, they're just regular women.

TOLIK

Yeah, right. Especially Aunt Shura. Beyonce, like.

*He walks to the fridge and pulls out a beer for himself and
another one for his brother. Both sit down on the couch.*

Valichka is bent over the pile of clothing in front of them. She is separating the lights and the darks.

TOLIK
　　Regular women, you say. Like, this one?

ANTON
　　Sure. A woman's a woman.

TOLIK
　　Are you serious?

ANTON
　　When she's turned like that—sure.

(He points at Valichka with his beer. She pays no attention to them.)

　　I kind of like ones like this... How do I put it...

TOLIK
　　Deaf-mute.

ANTON
　　No. Non-standard. There's something about it.

TOLIK
　　Right. Couldn't call for help if she were drowning, could she?

ANTON

That's not what I mean. You just... You never
understood women. You used to be afraid of
them, when you were little, remember?

TOLIK

I was afraid of nothing.

ANTON

(*laughs*)

No, you were. Remember, there was this woman
I knew, from the base? She was older than me.
Remember, I brought her home once, when
Mom was gone and the Old Man was gone,
and she stayed for the night with me, upstairs.
I came down in the middle of the night for a
drink of water, I was parched, and you ran after
me, crying. She scared you.

TOLIK

Dude, she was about to set me on fire! She
poured gasoline all over the place!

ANTON

So what? She wouldn't have lit it. She just had
too much to drink. It was a joke. And you got all
scared.

TOLIK

Like you wouldn't've if she'd doused you in
gasoline?

ANTON

No, I don't think I would. I understand women. Look at this one here, the way she stands—like a monument.

TOLIK

Like a tombstone.

ANTON

Like you would know. What's her name, do you know?

TOLIK

Valichka's her name. You want to talk to her now?

ANTON

What would be the point? Just grab her and drag her upstairs.

TOLIK

Right. To Mom's room.

ANTON

You moron.

Aunt Shura comes downstairs.

AUNT SHURA

Do you have a big bowl?

TOLIK
(*distracted, not looking at her*)
    A salad bowl, yeah.

AUNT SHURA
    That won't do. We need something bigger.
    Like a tub.

TOLIK
    You don't know what salads our Mom made.

ANTON
    Yeah.

AUNT SHURA
(*to Valichka who is standing above the pile of clothing*)
    Val', could you go look for something fitting?

VALICHKA
    Where?

AUNT SHURA
    In the kitchen somewhere, they'd have it there.

VALICHKA
    Alright.

The brothers, shocked, stare at Valichka. Valichka goes over to the fridge, looks around, finds a big metal bowl.

VALICHKA
    Like this?

AUNT SHURA

Like that. Let's go.

Valichka follows Aunt Shura up the stairs.

TOLIK

She's not deaf.

ANTON

Like hell she's not. She reads lips.

TOLIK

She heard us.

ANTON

What did she hear?

TOLIK

They'll rat us out.

ANTON

What should we do?

TOLIK

Whatever you want. Zhora'll show up with his crew tomorrow, and I'm done.

ANTON

Come on, Tokh'. Think about it. They are, like, the authorities, people elected them.

TOLIK

Let me tell you something about the people's choice. I wouldn't have let them vote, ever. You know how they vote? They vote thinking about their neighbor, not themselves.

ANTON

What do you mean?

TOLIK

I mean, whoever will make things worse for the neighbor—and the longer the better.

ANTON

What's with you and this Zhora-Sasha?

TOLIK

He's out to get me.

ANTON

Well, don't borrow money from him—he'll turn around.

TOLIK

You're a moron!

ANTON

No, you are!

They jump up, stand facing each other ready to fight.
   Upstairs, a door opens. Aunt Shura comes out first. She is carrying the bowl, filled with water, in her outstretched hands. The two other women follow, carrying bags of

clothes and things. They come down the stairs and walk across the room. Aunt Shura places the bowl on the table; the women set their bags on the floor, next to the pile of clothing. Aunt Shura stands at the table looking into the bowl. The two women come to flank her and look as well. Tolik and Anton come up quietly, stand behind Aunt Shura and peek into the bowl over her shoulder. Tolik turns away, disgusted. Anton begins to cry. Everyone is silent.

ANTON
Good God, Aunt Shura, what are we supposed to do now?

AUNT SHURA
We shall fast and pray.

ANTON
That's not what I meant. What about her things?

AUNT SHURA
You must give them away. They've no business lying around here. Valya and Katya will take them. Don't worry, Antosh'. Your late mother was like a sister to me, I washed her myself and I will see her off on her last journey.

TOLIK (*nervously*)
Aunt Shura, are you, like, done now? With washing, and everything?

AUNT SHURA
We have washed her.

TOLIK

Then okay, we can take it from here. You go ahead and go. Take the things. From the kitchen, whatever. And go ahead.

Aunt Shura sits down heavily. The women sit down on either side of her and press themselves against her. The brothers are forced to sit on the chairs on both sides of them.

AUNT SHURA
(*solemnly*)

It is you, Anton, I wish to speak to. You have always been a normal boy.

TOLIK
(*skeptically*)

Yeah, right.

AUNT SHURA
(*ignoring Tolik*)

You used to help your mother, I remember. Around the house.

TOLIK

Ha-ha...

AUNT SHURA

Your father was nothing much. You barely saw him. The whole place was on you, I remember. The garden, the vegetables.

TOLIK
> He's our young horticulturist.

AUNT SHURA
> I remember you helped fix your grandfather's place.

TOLIK
> I worked on that, too!

AUNT SHURA
(*can't stand it any longer and turns to Tolik*)
> You, Anatoly, burned that house down!

TOLIK
(*indignant*)
> What?

AUNT SHURA
> You did! Your grandfather's house.

TOLIK
> What! That wasn't me. He did it!

(*He points his finger at Anton.*)

AUNT SHURA
(*skeptically*)
> Ri-ight...

ANTON
> Aunt Shura...

AUNT SHURA (*to Anton*)
Be quiet!

(*She turns to Tolik.*)

You burned it down!

ANTON
Aunt Shura, the thing is...

AUNT SHURA
What?

ANTON
To tell the truth, it was me. Who burned it down.

TOLIK
(*laughs*)
Ah-a-a-a-a!

AUNT SHURA
(*confused*)
What do you mean, you did?

ANTON
Well, I did. Not on purpose, though.

TOLIK
Ah-ha-ha-ha! Horticulturist!

AUNT SHURA
(*turns sharply to Tolik*)
    Everyone still thinks it was you!

*Tolik stops laughing, confused. Aunt Shura, satisfied,
turns back to the bowl.*

AUNT SHURA
    Someone must sit up with her through the night.
    We'll stay and sit. We'll tidy here, too, and wash
    everything.

TOLIK
    Aunt Shura, you're like a cleaning service. What
    is it with you and the washing?

AUNT SHURA
(*to Anton*)
    I will speak with you. Your mother was like a
    sister to me. I'll get everything done right, don't
    you worry. Someone has to stay by her side. So
    her soul can find peace. You understand what
    I'm talking about?

ANTON
    Sure.

AUNT SHURA
    So we'll sit with her, don't you worry.

ANTON
    Alright, Aunt Shura.

TOLIK
Okay, listen up, Aunt Shura.

AUNT SHURA
(*to Anton*)
I'll just speak to you, don't you worry.

TOLIK
Aunt Shura!

AUNT SHURA
(*to Anton*)
We'll take care of everything, don't you worry,
Antosh'. For her soul to find peace.

TOLIK
Okay, ladies, look here! Let me tell you how
things are going to go here. Damn it, do you
hear me?

Everyone looks at Tolik, surprised.

TOLIK
Look here, ladies! Let's listen to me for a change.
You want to fast—you go ahead and knock
yourself out. We've nothing against that. But.
The three of you, you ladies, with the departed,
stay upstairs. I mean, with Mom. Tokha goes
upstairs, too, onto the mattress. I stay here, on
the couch. Is that clear?

ANTON
Why do I get the mattress?

TOLIK

You're welcome to sleep in the shower. Standing up. Like a penguin.

ANTON

You're the penguin!

TOLIK

Oh yeah? You tell me! Who's the penguin now?

AUNT SHURA
(*interrupts*)

You can't go upstairs, Anton. You should not be next to her. You are a kin soul, she won't find peace if you're near. You two sleep here, on the couch.

ANTON

I get the spot by the wall!

TOLIK

Hey!

AUNT SHURA

That's the right thing to do. We'll stay here until morning and bury her then. Then we'll see what's next.

TOLIK

We all know what's next.

AUNT SHURA

Last night, something burned all night on the far side of the river. They set something on fire. I worry about the fields catching.

ANTON

Well, the authorities must know. They'll deal with it. Sasha knows, right?

AUNT SHURA

Sasha?

ANTON

Sasha. The Mayor. Zhora.

AUNT SHURA

He's gone. Killed.

ANTON

What do you mean, killed?

AUNT SHURA

They killed him.

ANTON

Sasha?

AUNT SHURA

Yes.

TOLIK

What about Zhora?

AUNT SHURA
(*to Anton*)
> Listen. We'll stay here, sit with her. And you
> should stay here, too. That's the right thing to
> do, do you understand? So that her soul would
> find peace.

ANTON
> Sure, Aunt Shura, no problem. You go ahead,
> do what you need to do. I'll take care of things.
> Would you like some dinner?

AUNT SHURA
> It is that time, yes. We've got a lot of work to
> do, God willing.

ANTON
> We have canned food.

AUNT SHURA
> Uh-huh.

ANTON
(*points to the bowl*)
> What about this? Where should it go?

AUNT SHURA
> We'll clean this up. Valya, clean this up.

*Valichka gets up and takes the bowl out. She comes back,
sits down next to Anton. She studies his face intently.
Anton freezes at first, then springs into action.*

ANTON

Aunt Shura, you just sit there a minute, we'll take care of everything. You just sit. Tokha, come on, bring stuff over. Let's set the table. You just sit, Aunt Shura.

TOLIK

What am I now, a waiter?

ANTON
(*nervously*)

Come on, move.

(*He turns to Valichka.*)

You probably haven't eaten anything.

(*Loudly.*)

I said, you must be hungry!

TOLIK (*offended*)

Why are you shouting?

Tolik gets up, goes to the fridge, pulls out several bottles of beer and brings them back to the table. He opens them, one off another. Goes back to the fridge, brings breakfast cereal to the table, then empty bowls, then spoons. Makes another trip to the fridge and brings the cans of food. No one touches those. Finally, he sits down back on his chair, on the left flank of the women. Anton, meanwhile, keeps up the conversation.

ANTON
So, I'm saying, there I was, at the bridge, Aunt Shura. And they tell me, park your jeep here, Mister. Can you believe it?

AUNT SHURA
There is no bridge, Antosh'. It's gone. Got bombed a week ago.

ANTON
I do wonder, it's going to be some job to build it back, right? It was a good bridge, you could run semis over it.

AUNT SHURA
That bridge kept this whole place going. And they bombed it all to heck. God forgive.

TOLIK
Aunt Shura!

AUNT SHURA
(*not turning to look at him*)
What?

TOLIK
How are things downtown?

AUNT SHURA
Downtown? There's a war downtown, Tolya. Don't you watch TV?

TOLIK
I do, Aunt Shura. It just doesn't show anything.

AUNT SHURA
There's a war on, Tolya. Blood is spilled. The church stands empty.

TOLIK
Right, the priest joined the crusade, I heard. Aunt Shura!

AUNT SHURA
What?

TOLIK
Whose side are you on?

ANTON
Tokha!

TOLIK
I'm just curious is all.

ANTON
That's it, Tokha.

TOLIK
I don't mean anything by it. I'm just asking.

AUNT SHURA
I, Tolya, am on the side of there being no bloodshed. And for the church to open.

TOLIK
I see.

Everyone falls silent.

TOLIK
Aunt Shura.

AUNT SHURA
What?

TOLIK
The bridge is all gone, isn't it?

AUNT SHURA
So, what?

TOLIK
Then how the fuck did you get here? If the bridge is gone? Huh, ladies? How did you cross the river? Did you ford it?

The women, in silence, raise the bottles, drink their beers.

TOLIK
Come on, ladies, what's your story? Tell us how you crossed that river. 'Coz my idiot brother here just gave away his jeep to the people's representatives at the checkpoint.

ANTON
Come on, Tokha, alright already... Still, Aunt Shura, how did you manage the river?

TOLIK

Yes, Aunt Shura, do tell us. Did the priest teach you how to walk on water?

ANTON
(confused)

Aunt Shura?

Everyone looks at Aunt Shura. She holds the pause, then stands up, goes to the pile of clothes turned out of the wardrobe and starts picking through it, still silent. She sees the fur coat, picks it up, comes back to the table, and nods at the women to clear it. They put away the bowls and the spoons. Tolik makes a show of collecting the cans and putting them away in the fridge. Aunt Shura tosses the fur coat onto the table.

AUNT SHURA
(tenderly)

I remember this coat. This one here. You know where it came from? You were too little, you wouldn't remember. I gave it to her, as a present. For her birthday. It was winter, freezing cold, and she went around in her raincoat. You know, she never bought anything for herself, she spent everything she had on you. I remember I came to the post office, and there she was, outside, waiting for it to open after the lunchbreak, so she could go get the money someone had sent her. And she says to me: Shura, I won't survive this winter, I'll freeze to death. Look after the boys, she says. I went straight home, got this fur coat, and brought it back to her. Here, I said,

you raise your own boys, quit freezing. She wore
it until she died. And look—it's still like new.
They burned down the post office last week.

ANTON
What do you mean, burned down?

AUNT SHURA
You know, doused it with gasoline one night and
set it on fire. It was a strategic target, they said,
better to burn it down. I went there on Sunday,
and there was our mailman, the scary one,
Mongol-looking, you know?

TOLIK
Yeah, I know him.

AUNT SHURA
He was just standing there with his mail bag.
Just standing there, crying.

TOLIK
No kidding? That guy—crying?

AUNT SHURA
Crying. I says to him, don't cry, what's there to
cry about. Should've burned that old barrack
long time ago. And he says to me: and what am
I supposed to do now? How am I to go on? With
no post office, he says, what am I to do now?
And what am I supposed to tell him? Go home, I
says. Come back after the war. So he dropped his
bag and went.

Everyone falls silent again.

ANTON
I used to love that post office. I used to run there when I was a kid. Remember that, Tokh'?

TOLIK
Sure, I went with you, remember?

ANTON
Right. Well, where else did we have to go?

TOLIK
Yep. We'd run there first thing in the morning and wait for the truck to bring the mail.

ANTON
Right. Remember that one time you fell asleep there, right in the street?

TOLIK
Yep. In winter.

ANTON
Right. I thought you froze to death.

TOLIK
Well, I did, didn't I?

ANTON
Right!

TOLIK

Yep!

The two of them laugh.

ANTON

I mean, I thought you froze all the way. Dead.

Everyone falls silent.

TOLIK

You know, to be honest, I kind of wanted
to burn it down myself, that post office.
Honestly. I did.

AUNT SHURA

Well, it's gone now. The mailman is still there,
but no mail.

ANTON

And the fur-coat is still here. Mom's coat. Aunt
Shura, you, if you would like it, you should take
it. Something to remember Mom by.

AUNT SHURA

Yes, dear, don't worry, I'll take it. You don't
worry about anything, we'll clean things up
here, make it all nice and tidy.

ANTON

Thank you, Aunt Shura. We'll help you. We'll
sort it out, right, Tokha?

TOLIK

Sure thing.

AUNT SHURA

No need, Antosh', we'll manage, don't you worry. You just do what you've been doing.

(Turns to Valichka and says loudly:)

Clean up here! We'll do the upstairs!

Aunt Shura gets up, claps the woman next to her on the shoulder, and the woman gets up, too. They go upstairs. At the table, Valichka remains sitting, flanked by Tolik and Anton. The brothers study Valichka closely.

ANTON

Valichka, did you have something to eat? Have more.

Valichka is silent.

ANTON

No? Would you like something more?

(He turns to Tolik.)

She can't hear. How are we supposed to talk to her?

TOLIK

What are you going to talk to her about, Tokh'?

ANTON
The weather.

TOLIK
She won't hear you about the weather, Tokh'.
She's deaf.

ANTON
That's a shame. She's a nice one.

(*He turns to Valichka.*)

I say, you are a right good woman. You need
a man, is what you need.

*Valichka emphatically picks up her beer and takes a drink.
She gets up and goes to wash the dishes.*

ANTON
Right. Deaf.

(*He picks up the fur coat, puts it on.*)

Nothing wrong with this fur coat. Re-cut it, it'll
last forever yet.

*Tolik quickly moves to sit next to his brother, hugs
him around the shoulders, and, glancing nervously at
Valichka, speaks.*

TOLIK
Tokh,' I'm telling you, someone sent them.

ANTON
> Oh, come on.

TOLIK
> They're here for a reason. Someone'll show up tomorrow, and they'll turn us right in.

ANTON
> Tokh', they don't even talk! Look at this one: she doesn't talk. Valichka!

Valichka continues to wash the dishes, showing no reaction.

TOLIK
(grabs his brother by the shoulders again and whispers)
> Right. She's not talking to you, you moron. With Comrade Mayor she talks like he's family. Tells him everything. Everything she saw, everything she heard. They are here for a reason. They've come to get *me*, don't you see?

ANTON
> What'd they want you for?

TOLIK
> And what do they want here, period? Bury our Mom? Aunt Shura never even came to visit. I haven't seen her in a million years. And this coat...

(He grabs Anton by the collar.)

She told a right pretty story here—fur this, and fur that... So what? You look like a beaver in it.

ANTON
(*pushes his brother away*)
You are the beaver! Asshole.

He jumps to his feet, goes to the fridge, and pulls out two beers. Opens one against the other, and shoves one bottle at Valichka. She looks surprised but accepts the beer. She puts down the dishes, takes a drink. Anton grabs a spoon from the sink and uses it to open his own beer. Drops the spoon back into the sink, and picks up a knife. Stands there, holding a beer in one hand and the knife in the other. Decisively, he clinks his bottle against Valichka's.

ANTON
Here, Valichka, let's drink to our mom's immortal soul, may it rest in peace. She was a treasure, I tell you that. No other Mom like her anywhere in the whole world. But, seeing as you can't hear for fuck, I won't elaborate. Go ahead, drink up, love. Happy New Year!

Valichka nods in understanding. The two take a drink. Tolik jumps to his feet and runs up to his brother. Now the three of them are standing at the fridge, Valichka in the middle, and Anton and Tolik on either side of her.

TOLIK
Dude, do you really not get it? They'll carry us both out tomorrow. Feet first. With Mom.

ANTON
Don't holler—Valichka will hear you.

TOLIK
Valichka is deaf.

ANTON
She can read lips.

Anton crouches.

ANTON
Bend down.

Tolik crouches next to him. Valichka looks at them from above, takes another drink.

ANTON
Ok, I'm with you. What's your plan?

TOLIK
The plan? We've got to get them out of here.

ANTON
What about Mom?

TOLIK
We keep Mom.

ANTON
Dude! I mean, what do we do about Mom? Her soul won't find peace.

TOLIK
Fine. It'll hang around for a while and then leave.

ANTON
But they're set to stay the night. To do it right.

TOLIK
Yeah, I see. You want her

(*he nods at Valichka*)

to stay the night, don't you?

ANTON
Where'd you get that idea?

TOLIK
Look, the fur on your fur coat is all stood up.

ANTON
Get to the point. What are we doing? We can't just throw them out.

TOLIK
Why not?

ANTON
Because, one, she reads lips. She's already lip-read everything she needs, dude. You've talked enough to get ten years with confiscation of property.

TOLIK

So?

ANTON

And two, let them clean the place. We can always throw them out later. Here's what I think: let them spend the night upstairs, with Mom. I'll sleep here with you. Once they are asleep, you and I will get up quietly and get rid of all the shit you have squirreled away here. Anyone wants to search the place—it's clean. Right?

TOLIK

Right. Except this one small thing.

ANTON

What small thing?

TOLIK

They didn't come here to sleep. They'll stay up all night with her, like a picnic. So you ain't getting rid of nothing.

ANTON

Well, we'll just have to see. Don't you worry, Tokh'. I'm gonna solve this.

He turns to Valichka.

ANTON

So, Valichka, you ladies will be sleeping upstairs, right?

Valichka says nothing and looks at him sarcastically.

ANTON
Read my lips! Where are you going to sleep?

Valichka says nothing.

ANTON
Sleep!

Tolik rushes closer, speaks into Valichka's face.

TOLIK
D'you hear him, lady?

ANTON
Valichka, I'm asking if...

TOLIK
Read his lips!

ANTON
You can't hear me, can you?

TOLIK
Hey!

ANTON
She can't hear. You try.

TOLIK
Listen up, lady! My brother is asking where you're planning to sleep?

ANTON

> Read his lips!

TOLIK

> I repeat: where—will you—sleep?

ANTON

> Read his lips!

TOLIK

> I've asked you a frigging question!

ANTON

> Okay, don't read now.

Anton grabs Tolik, drags him back to the couch, sits him down and sits down next to him. With a one-armed hug he keeps his brother firmly in place.

ANTON

> Alright, bro, you chill. Sit down and chill. Sit down and just sit here, d'you hear me?

TOLIK

> Yeah, yeah.

ANTON

> I mean, did you hear me?

TOLIK

> I did already! It's fine, let me go.

ANTON

You just sit right here. You got it?

TOLIK

Yes.

ANTON

Good. You just sit and think.

The brothers sit on the couch for a while, silent, thinking.
Valichka resumes her work. The house is quiet. Upstairs,
the door to the mother's bedroom opens. Aunt Shura,
unnoticed by others, quietly comes out onto the landing.
She stands on the edge of the steps, peers carefully
downstairs, listens. Then, just as quietly, she slips back
into the room and shuts the door behind her.

III

Never a sign nor a trace of you. I want every memory of you to stun like a physical blow, to reverberate everywhere, to cause pain and suffering. I want to go blind with the knowledge that I can't see your footprint on the moist earth in the morning, can't answer your morning greeting, can't touch your shoulder still warm from sleep.

Never again have I listened to such even breathing, never have I witnessed an awakening such as yours when the whole world is a great, good day that holds still waiting for you, watches faithfully over your dreams, and then rushes into your bed, into your arms as soon as you are awake and fawns upon you, spins and leaps with joy, telling everything around that you are now here.

The warm world of your words and whispers, the world of gossamer and the cooling greenery outside our window, the world of trust, of confessing our deepest secrets, the world of sadness, of the black void—it sinks like an ice floe in March, grows darker with the coming of the night, does not answer, does not call back...

*The time is late at night. The house is dark.
Downstairs, TOLIK and ANTON lie on the couch,
their backs against each other. The door upstairs
opens, and AUNT SHURA emerges, carrying a
lit candle. She comes to the top of the stairs and
stands there, listening. After a while, she goes back
to the room, closing the door behind her.*

TOLIK
(*in a low voice*)
Tokh'...

ANTON
What?

TOLIK
You asleep?

ANTON
No.

TOLIK
Did you hear her? She is walking up there,
listening.

ANTON
So?

TOLIK
What are we going to do?

ANTON
Nothing. They'll go to sleep eventually.

TOLIK

Yeah, right. They are like zombies. Now's about high noon for them.

ANTON

Don't worry about it. (*He turns to the other side.*) What are you so worked up about? Just chill.

TOLIK

Tokh'...

ANTON

What?

TOLIK

Move your arm.

Anton, embarrassed, turns back to his original side. Silence.

ANTON

What was it like here?

TOLIK

Meaning?

ANTON

When it all started, what was it like? Gunfights?

TOLIK

Not at first. They took over everything downtown and put up checkpoints. But they didn't shoot. Who'd they shoot at around here?

ANTON

Fair point. And then?

TOLIK

And then it started. No one had any clue,
at first, what to do. So they're shooting—let
them shoot at each other. A pal of mine here,
he drove a taxi, took people across, through
the checkpoints. Under fire, too. Did that for
a whole month, just think.

ANTON

And then?

TOLIK

They burned him. His own people. I mean, our
people. You know what I mean.

ANTON

Did many sign up to fight?

TOLIK

Yeah, they did, at first. Then they came back.

ANTON

You signed up to be a sniper, didn't you? For the
good of the Christian cause?

TOLIK

I didn't sign up for nothing.

ANTON

Where'd you get that rifle from then?

TOLIK
Quiet.

ANTON
What do you mean, quiet?

TOLIK
Quiet.

The door upstairs open and Aunt Shura comes out. She blows out her candle and stands listening. Then she goes back into the room.

ANTON
She ain't sleeping.

TOLIK
They say, she turned people in.

ANTON
How do you mean?

TOLIK
You know, how. When the whole thing just started, they say she went in with a list. And there were twelve people on it.

ANTON
Who says that?

TOLIK
People.

ANTON

People who, like, seen this list?

TOLIK

How should I know? I'm telling you what I heard.

ANTON

And I heard she fed the men at the checkpoints. Like, took them meals and stuff. And someone reported her to the Commandant's office. And she paid them off somehow. That's what I've been told.

TOLIK

Aunt Shura?

ANTON

Yeah.

TOLIK

Fed people?

ANTON

That's what I heard.

TOLIK

Poison mushrooms maybe.

Anton turns to the other side, faces Tolik.

ANTON

Well, you can't tell who's on whose side anymore. You talk to a person and you have no clue what she has in her head. Better not to talk at all.

TOLIK
Yeah.

ANTON
Here, you tell me: people signed up and then came back. And where I am, half of our people picked up and left—didn't want to hang around these types here.

TOLIK
Then why didn't Aunt Shura leave?

ANTON
Hell knows. She's got her church here.

TOLIK
Dude, it's not like it's the only church in the world, is it? What's she like—couldn't go to church somewhere quieter?

ANTON
I suppose she could've... Listen, you're the one who knows her. What's this you worry about: she'll turn us in? She won't turn anyone in.

Tolik says nothing.

ANTON
And she didn't turn anyone in to the Commandant's either. She's Christian. Orthodox.

That's a sin for them: to turn anyone in to the Commandant's. D'you hear me?

Tolik still says nothing.

ANTON
Hey, why aren't you saying anything?

TOLIK
Move your arm.

(*He pauses.*)

Seems like they've gone quiet.

ANTON
They have?

TOLIK
Yep. Come on.

Tolik and Anton get up quietly, flip up the couch and pull out the rifle. Tolik carefully walks to the door, Anton follows. They freeze there, listening. In the silence, someone loudly knocks on the door from outside. Tolik tosses the rifle into the wardrobe.

ANTON
Who's there?

MAN'S VOICE
C'mon, open up!

ANTON
>Who is it?

MAN'S VOICE
>It's Kolya, your neighbor! Open up!

Tolik opens the door using his phone as a light. Anton does the same. KOLYA sort of falls in. Kolya is substantial, even sort of fat. He is dressed in a pair of overalls and rubber boots. He speaks loudly. He is also using his cell phone as a light. Behind him, he is dragging his wife, MASHKA. Mashka is wrapped in a warm, fuzzy robe and wears Micky Mouse slippers. She carries a large plastic shopping bag.

KOLYA
(*to Mashka*)
>Here, come over here, sit.

He seats her at the table.

KOLYA
(*to Tolik*)
>You got something to drink?

TOLIK
>We've got beer.

KOLYA
>I'm not drinking right now. The harvest.
>Mashka, you want some?

MASHKA
>I do.

KOLYA
(*to Tolik*)
  She won't have any either.

All sit down around Mashka. Kolya is anxious and aggressive.

KOLYA
  Mashka's having a baby.

TOLIK
  How do you mean?

KOLYA
  I mean, she's about to pop.

(*He points to Mashka.*)

  To have the baby. She's got the contractions.

MASHKA
  Jesssus Christ, I've got no such thing, why d'you have to make things up?

KOLYA
  Mash', not now. I can see what's happening. We gotta get you to the hospital.

MASHKA
  Jesssus, what would you do there?

KOLYA
  We'll have the baby.

MASHKA

Kolya, you're like a child, I swear.

KOLYA

Mash'!

ANTON

Whom are you expecting?

KOLYA

The ambulance. Except we ain't about to see it. The bridge is gone.

ANTON

Yep, it's gone.

KOLYA

Do you have a car?

ANTON

My car's gone, too. I left it at the checkpoint, on the other side.

KOLYA

So here's the thing: my jeep croaked, all other machinery is in the fields, I've got this harvest to bring in, and she's having a baby.

MASHKA

Kolya!

KOLYA

Not now, Mash'! Like I said. Tolik, do something.
She's about to pop, I swear. We have to take her
downtown. To call another ambulance. I don't
know what.

TOLIK

What do you think I can do? What am I,
a midwife? Why'd you come here?

KOLYA

Where else am I supposed to go? There's no
one left around here: you with your Mom, and
Mashka and me.

TOLIK

Mom is gone now.

KOLYA

She left?

TOLIK

She left... She died, our Mom.

KOLYA
(*businesslike*)
I see. How long?

TOLIK

Yesterday.

KOLYA

I see. And where is she?

ANTON
Upstairs.

KOLYA
What?

ANTON
Upstairs.

KOLYA
How do you mean, upstairs?

ANTON
I mean she's upstairs, in her room.

KOLYA
(*nods in that direction*)
Like, there?

Upstairs, a door creaks open. Aunt Shura emerges, carrying a candle. She blows out the candle and stands there, listening.

KOLYA
Is that her?

TOLIK
That's Aunt Shura. It's a girls' night.

KOLYA
What do you mean?

ANTON
They are sitting with the recently departed.

TOLIK
So that her soul would find peace.

MASHKA
Kol', I'm afraid of the dead. I'm so scared I might actually go ahead and go into labor.

KOLYA
Not now, Mash', not now.

(*He speaks to Tolik in a low voice.*)

Aunt Shura? Are you for real? It's her?

ANTON
Herself. Why?

KOLYA
(*starts laughing*)
Did you know they are looking for her?

ANTON
Who?

KOLYA
There's a flier with her face at the post office. Wanted.

TOLIK
Did she kill someone?

KOLYA
I wouldn't put it past her. Why'd you let her in?

ANTON
She came to wash Mom. The dead.

MASHKA
Kol', I'm scared.

KOLYA
(*to Mashka*)
Quiet!

(*He then turns to the brothers.*)

For real? She washed your Mom? What if she also, you know...

ANTON
Are you insane?

KOLYA
You are! Why do you think they're looking for her? I've been wanting to see her myself, for a while. I want to ask her something.

ANTON
About what?

KOLYA
About the political situation in our country.

ANTON

Kol', don't start.

KOLYA

Why shouldn't I? What if you're on the lam right with her?

ANTON

I'm not on the lam. I came to help bury Mom. We've called a car. It's coming in the morning.

KOLYA

Sure, we'll bury her. We'll help—what else are neighbors for? We'll sort it all out, Tokha, don't you worry.

TOLIK

Shit.

KOLYA

We'll sort it all out.

(*Loudly.*)

Aunt Shura?! Hey, Aunt Shura?!

Aunt Shura comes downstairs. Everyone falls silent. Aunt Shura studies the group: the men with their cell phones now turned off and Mashka with her plastic bag.

AUNT SHURA

Mashka? What's wrong?

ANTON
> She's in labor, Aunt Shura.

MASHKA
> You are all in labor, you morons!

AUNT SHURA
> In labor? How long?

KOLYA
> She needs to get to the hospital. Downtown.

ANTON
> But the bridge is gone.

KOLYA
> They blew the bridge up. Didn't they,
> Aunt Shura?

AUNT SHURA
> They did, they did. Ok, let's have her lie down.

(She turns to Mashka.)

> You need to lie down. I'll go outside, look
> for water.

KOLYA
(goes and stands by the door)
> Here's what I think: No one is going anywhere.
> Everyone stays right here until morning. When
> the car comes, we'll let them sort it all out.

AUNT SHURA

What if the baby comes before then?

MASHKA

I am not having any babies here with you. I get it, Kolya's off with his harvest stuff, but you, Aunt Shura? How am I supposed to talk to them? They're like children. Retarded ones!

KOLYA

Baby comes, we'll raise it. Nobody's going anywhere.

TOLIK

Kolya, are you fucking nuts? Get away from the door.

KOLYA

I said, no one's going anywhere.

He pulls a hand grenade out of his pocket.

MASHKA

Kolya! Oh God, here it comes.

KOLYA

Nothing comes. I said, everyone stay put.

MASHKA

I mean, the baby! It's actually coming.

KOLYA

Mash', can you please not now, okay?

MASHKA

What do you mean not now, Kolya?

KOLYA

Just—later. Can't you see what's going on here?

MASHKA

Kolya, you fucking moron, I'm in fucking labor.

KOLYA

I said: not now.

TOLIK

You're one clown, Kolya. Your woman's having a baby and you run around with a grenade in your pants.

KOLYA

Are you all in together? Is that it? Did you all know they're looking for her?

TOLIK

You moron.

(*He turns to Mashka.*)

Okay, here, lie down on the couch. Aunt Shura, can you do a baby? Or are you about the dead only?

AUNT SHURA

There's nothing to do about the baby. She needs a blanket or something. And someone has to get water.

KOLYA

What water? No one is going anywhere. I'm calling the Commandant's office.

TOLIK

Listen, dude, who asked you here?

KOLYA

Tol', I don't get it. Whose side are you on?

TOLIK

Like I would fucking tell you. Get it?

KOLYA

Tolik, don't mess with me! You don't get it. She's on the lam. Whose side are you on?

Tolik slowly approaches Kolya.

TOLIK

Give me the grenade.

KOLYA

Tolyan, don't do this! You don't understand.

TOLIK

The grenade, now!

He grabs Kolya's hand and silently attempts to wrestle the grenade from him. Kolya resists. For a while, they pull the grenade back and forth. Finally, Tolik wrests it from Kolya, walks away to the refrigerator and stands there panting. He opens the fridge and puts the grenade inside.

TOLIK
Fucking moron.

Aunt Shura helps Mashka to the couch and makes her lie down. Anton covers Mashka with the fur coat.

AUNT SHURA
You just need to calm down now. Rest here. The car's coming. The hearse.

MASHKA
Kolya, I'm scared!

AUNT SHURA
Don't be scared. The car will come, and we'll take you to the hospital, and you'll have your baby just fine.

(She turns to Kolya.)

Everyone does, and you will. Nothing to be scared about.

MASHKA
I won't ride in the car with a corpse.

TOLIK

That would be my Mom, actually.

MASHKA

Tol', I've always been very good to your Mom. When she was alive, I mean. She was my neighbor, right? You just try to see it from my point of view: how am I to ride with her in my condition? Plus, Kolya's gone psycho.

TOLIK

Shouldn't have married him then.

MASHKA

When I married him, he was normal. It's all his farming. I'm actually sorry for him. Kind of. Maybe.

TOLIK

Of course, I get it, Mash'! It's fine. We'll have the car take you first. Just as soon as they can get here.

MASHKA

You think they will?

TOLIK

Ask your man there. He seems to have pals in the Commandant's office, maybe he can call them. They'll tell him.

Kolya sits down on the floor, his back against the door, wraps his arms around his head and starts to cry.

KOLYA
(*raises his head*)
> What pals, Tokha? Why are you like that? We've
> lived our whole lives together. Why are you
> being like that?

TOLIK
> Alright already.

KOLYA
(*to Mashka*)
> And you, too. I told you, didn't I, a month ago,
> I told you: let's leave, you'll have your baby
> in peace, we'll wait things out and come back
> later. But now, you had to have us sitting in the
> basement, didn't you?

MASHKA
> You wouldn't leave that basement! You've got all
> your canning down there.

AUNT SHURA
(*to Kolya*)
> Don't yell at her. She can't be stressed.

KOLYA
> And you, Aunt Shura—you're the one to talk.
> Who do you think you are, a fucking hero? Zoya
> fucking Kosmodemyanskaya? I don't know what
> all you've done, but something tells me they are
> not looking for you to give you a peace prize.

AUNT SHURA
(*to Mashka*)
> Don't mind him. Men'll say anything at the
> moment.

KOLYA
> Sure they will. Everyone now knows what to
> do, everyone has a plan, don't they? They are all
> politicians now. Take you, Aunt Shura, you know
> all about politics, right?

AUNT SHURA
> I know nothing.

KOLYA
> Right, like hell you do. Who started all this? Back
> then, in the spring? Who did it? Me? I had the
> planting to do, I had no time for politics. I, Aunt
> Shura, am a farmer. I feed you all.

AUNT SHURA
> You ought to go to church, Kolya.

KOLYA
> I, Aunt Shura, fixed your goddamn church.
> Tithed, you could say, my own labor. So?
> Where's our priest now?

TOLIK
> He's at war, our pastor. Out to recover the
> Church of the Holy Sepulcher.

KOLYA

Oh yeah? From whom? Who took it from him? And why did they blow up our bridge? You tell me, Aunt Shura, what the church says about damaging public infrastructure.

AUNT SHURA

Kolya, you are an idiot.

KOLYA

(*sobbing again*)

Sure, I'm the idiot. Take you, Anton, you are an educated man, you work at the market. Do you understand politics?

ANTON

I do not.

KOLYA

And you don't go to the rallies, do you?

ANTON

No, I don't.

KOLYA

Then who the fuck does? Every time you turn on the TV, there's a hell of a lot of people with icons in front of the mayor's office. Enough to make your tap water holy. Who are they then? Do you know, Anton?

ANTON

I do not.

KOLYA

And neither do I. What a strange war we've got ourselves here, then! Can't have a baby properly, and can't bury a person. We're just sitting here, like mice in a trap. And no one's done anything.

TOLIK

Speak for yourself.

KOLYA

And why is that, Tokha? What's wrong with me?

TOLIK

I don't remember you objecting much when all this started.

KOLYA

Yeah? Well, I, Tokh', did not have much free time to raise objections and such. I had fertilizer to spread. And your goddamn church to fix.

TOLIK

Right. And sand to take to the checkpoints, right?

KOLYA

What sand?

TOLIK

The people's sand. From the sand pit. Don't pretend you don't know now, Kol'!

KOLYA
(offended)
> I never took anything... (*He then addresses
> everyone.*) I could care less about this war of
> yours, mind you. I've got the crop ready and
> can't bring it in.

ANTON
> But we've got the truce now. For the harvest.
> So go pick your wheat.

KOLYA
> D'you think it's like mushrooms or something?
> "Pick" he says. I'm a week out of diesel. My
> machinery's all stuck. While you fight your war.

AUNT SHURA
> And the fields been burning. Two days already.
> Forget your harvest.

KOLYA
> What do you mean, burning?

AUNT SHURA
> There's fire coming from the river. You can see it
> well from above.

KOLYA
(*to Tolik*)
> What does she mean, from the river? Mind if
> I take a look?

TOLIK

Not at all. Just remember: Mom's there.

MASHKA

Kolya, don't go.

KOLYA

So what, Mom. She won't bite me, will she?

TOLIK

Not anymore.

*Kolya gets to his feet and sees the key in the door.
He turns it to lock the door and puts it emphatically
into his pocket.*

KOLYA

Everyone stays here. Is that clear?

TOLIK

Moron.

KOLYA

I'm gonna go look.

MASHKA

Kolya, don't.

KOLYA

I'll only be a sec, don't worry.

MASHKA

Jesssus Christ.

Kolya runs up the stairs lighting his way with his cell phone. He opens the door to the room.

KOLYA
Oh, hi…

He closes the door and runs back downstairs.

KOLYA
Who's that up there?

TOLIK
Aunt Shura's choir.

ANTON
For Mom.

TOLIK
So her soul would find peace.

ANTON
But they can't hear anything, don't worry.

KOLYA
Who said I was?

Kolya runs up the stairs again, opens the door, and enters the room leaving the door ajar. We see nothing but can hear him.

KOLYA
(*shouts*)
Tokha!

TOLIK
What?

KOLYA
Mind if I take a picture?

TOLIK
Of who?

KOLYA
Of your Mom.

TOLIK
Why?

KOLYA
Well, you know... To remember her by...

TOLIK
(*runs up the stairs as well*)
Are you fucking nuts? What are you, taking a
selfie with her? When your Mom dies, then be
my guest, take all kinds of pictures. Get out
of there. And you, too, clear out, let the room
breathe a little.

KOLYA
Look—the fire. It is from the river, like she said.

TOLIK
I see it.

KOLYA

Everything's gonna burn. That's my land there.

TOLIK

Tough luck with the harvest.

KOLYA

What do you mean, tough luck? Who's going to pay me? I'm all in. The diesel alone.

TOLIK

Well, you heard—they took my bro's car. And he's ok.

ANTON

(*from downstairs*)

No one took anything. I'll get it back. We'll sort it out.

TOLIK

Right. They'll give Kolyan here a new harvester, too. For his pioneering innovations. Right, Kolya?

KOLYA

Fuck you.

He runs down the stairs. Valichka and Katya also come down and stand beside Aunt Shura. Aunt Shura is whispering something above Mashka and pays no attention to others. Kolya sits down at the table and buries his head in his hands. Anton produces a couple of beers from the fridge, opens them, sits down next to Kolya, and shares a beer with him. Tolik is the last to leave the room upstairs. He remains on the landing, listening to the conversation below.

KOLYA

I just don't get it. Why would anyone burn the wheat? Alright, they're shooting at each other. Alright, they blow up checkpoints. They've got their war to do, I get it, I'm all for it. But why burn the wheat?

ANTON

You say it like they set your field on fire on purpose.

KOLYA

And even if they didn't—d'you think they give a shit? D'you think if I go to the Commandant's office tomorrow and file a complaint, what do you think they'll say to that? They'll pack me off to dig trenches.

TOLIK

And you'll go. Tell me you won't.

ANTON

(*to Tolik*)
Don't start.

TOLIK

Why not? What is he here, Mother Teresa? He says he had fertilizer to put in. How about he tells us where he got that grenade?

KOLYA
(*angry*)
　　I bought it.

TOLIK
　　Right. At the market. Tokha, how much are
　　grenades going for these days?

ANTON
　　We don't sell grenades.

TOLIK
　　Tough luck with the harvest, eh?

KOLYA
(*jumps to his feet, runs to the bottom of the stairs*)
　　And to hear you say it, you've never seen
　　a grenade before. But if I were to look around
　　here, I'd find a thing or two just the same. Say
　　I wouldn't.

TOLIK
(*angry*)
　　Go ahead, be my guest.

KOLYA
　　You bet I will.

TOLIK
　　So go ahead.

KOLYA
　　What are you, scared?

TOLIK
Of what? You?

KOLYA
Sure, me.

Kolya climbs a few stairs and Tolik comes a few stairs down. Tolik looms over Kolya.

MASHKA
Kolya! Kolya, stop it.

KOLYA
Mash', not now.

MASHKA
Kolya!

KOLYA
You heard me.

Aunt Shura gets up and comes to stand in the middle of the room. Valichka and Katya stand behind her.

AUNT SHURA
The time is now for everyone to be silent. Be silent and listen. Tolik, that's your mother upstairs. In the morning, they'll take her away and you won't see her again. Not ever. But at the moment, she is here. I suggest you go sit with her for a bit.

TOLIK

Aunt Shura, there's nothing to breathe in there.

AUNT SHURA

It's no different down here. It's the smoke. Everything's going to burn. (*She turns to Tolik and Kolya.*) Listen to me: let Mashka sleep a while, she needs her rest. Come sit down, both of you. You can talk later.

TOLIK

We've got nothing to talk about.

(*He turns to Kolya.*)

Get out of my way, you fucking farmer.

Tolik walks around Kolya, comes to the table, and sits down next to his brother. Aunt Shura and the other women also take seats at the table. Kolya comes, too, and looks for a place to sit, but there are no chairs left. Anton gets up, goes to the fridge, gets two fistfuls of beers, comes back, and puts the bottles on the table. Then he goes back to the fridge, pulls out the grenade and hands it to Tolik.

ANTON

Here.

TOLIK

(*takes it*)

What am I supposed to do with it? Here, farmer, you take it. Keep on fighting, whoever's side you are on.

Kolya takes the grenade hesitantly, weighs it in his hand, then firmly puts it down on the table.

KOLYA

I've no need of it. Tokh', don't be mad. I came here 'coz you are my neighbors.

TOLIK

Right. And brought the grenade.

KOLYA

It's the stress. Mashka there is having a baby. Everything's on fire. And we're stuck here with no way out. Don't be mad, okay?

TOLIK

Fine.

KOLYA

You know I've always been good to you. Ever since that accident... Well, since all that happened. With your Anna. You know what I mean.

TOLIK

Don't start.

ANTON

Don't go there.

KOLYA

But I don't mean it like that. We were all worried sick about you back then.

TOLIK

Alright already.

KOLYA

Okay, I'll stop. I just wanted to say it. So that you'd know.

TOLIK

I know.

ANTON

We know, Kolya. Thank you.

KOLYA

Right. None of us knew what to do when all that happened. Who could have thought...

AUNT SHURA

We're all here by the grace of God. I've outlived everyone in this street already. Your mom was the last. Everyone's gone. I'll go, too. I'll bury her and go.

ANTON

You are still young, Aunt Shura.

AUNT SHURA

I know everything about everyone here. I have seen everyone die. I watched this street empty out. Unless the war ends, you will all leave. Once there was a street—and now it's gone. It's history.

TOLIK
I'm not going anywhere.

AUNT SHURA
You are going first. You can't stay here.

TOLIK
And why is that?

AUNT SHURA
You know why.

KOLYA
Tolik, what's that about?

TOLIK
Nothing.

AUNT SHURA
Nothing. (*She turns to Kolya.*) You can't stay either.

KOLYA
What have I done?

AUNT SHURA
When the new government comes, they'll remember what you did for the checkpoints.

KOLYA
I, Aunt Shura, am a small man. I did what I was told.

ANTON

Ha-ha! You're one slimy one. Ha.

AUNT SHURA

And you, Antosha, better not go back to your market.

ANTON

Alright already!

TOLIK

Why is that bro? You got them sand, too?

ANTON

I did nothing. And you, Aunt Shura, instead of declaring us all here dead, better tell us about the bridge.

AUNT SHURA

What bridge? There is no bridge.

ANTON

Right. The bridge is gone. But you are here. Which means there must be a ford or something, right? Here's why I'm asking: I just need to know, are they coming in the morning or not.

AUNT SHURA

They are.

ANTON

And how do you know that?

AUNT SHURA

Trust me, Antosha. I know everything.

KOLYA

You're a witch, Aunt Shura. He asked you like
a human.

AUNT SHURA

Don't cuss at me. And take your bomb away.

*Kolya reluctantly picks up the grenade and shoves it into
his pocket.*

TOLIK

So, basically, as I understand it, come morning,
they won't just take Mom. They'll take all of us.

ANTON

I've got nothing to do with this.

TOLIK

Sure, sure.

KOLYA

Right, you just happened to stop by.
Right, Tokha?

(He laughs at Tolik.)

TOLIK

Not even related.

KOLYA
Ha-ha-ha.

AUNT SHURA
Be quiet now. You'll wake Mashka.

The candle Aunt Shura had placed on the table slowly sputters out.

AUNT SHURA
There goes the candle.

Tolik, Anton, and Kolya pull out their cell phones, turn on the flashlights, and put the phones on the table. The lights of the phones light the ceiling like searchlights.

TOLIK
And the fucking phones are running out.

KOLYA
And no one's called.

ANTON
They won't.

TOLIK
In that case, let them run.

AUNT SHURA
It'll be light soon. It's summer, the nights are short. Here's what I think we should do: as soon as it's light, we'll take Mashka and go to the bridge. We can try to think of what's next there.

TOLIK

And what will be next?

AUNT SHURA

We'll see. We can't stay here anyway. We'll all burn.

TOLIK

She won't make it. It's a hike from here.

AUNT SHURA

God willing, she will.

TOLIK

Right. Aunt Shura?

AUNT SHURA

What?

TOLIK

Aunt Shura, do you really believe in God?

AUNT SHURA

Why do you ask?

TOLIK

It's just, things are kind of fucked up for you. Not the way they're supposed to be. You go to church. Set our priest on his crusade and all. You, like, know all these different prayers by heart. And I look at you—and things are not going well. Why is that, Aunt Shura?

KOLYA

Leave it, Tokh'. It's not like you're king of the hill,
either.

TOLIK

But I never even aspired. Did I ever tithe? No. I'm
a private citizen, not listed in church. And you all
are righteous here, aren't you? And now what?
It's your crop burning out there.

AUNT SHURA

It's not about the crops. Everything's on fire.
For the private people and the righteous, all the
same. You tell me, which one was your mom?

TOLIK

My mom was a woman with a very difficult lot
in life.

AUNT SHURA

So, not a righteous one, was she?

TOLIK

To put it mildly.

AUNT SHURA

But she never did anything downright ungodly,
did she?

TOLIK

That depends how you looked at it.

AUNT SHURA

So look at it honestly.

TOLIK

Honestly, Aunt Shura, she was kind of like you: no one loved her very much, but everyone sent greetings each holiday. On the other hand, who here loves anyone especially much?

KOLYA

God loves everybody. Right, Aunt Shura?

AUNT SHURA

Not even close.

All fall silent.

ANTON

Not the most stimulating conversation, is it? Ladies, maybe you could share something interesting?

TOLIK

Right, they'll read you your rights in unison. Only you'll have to read their lips.

ANTON

Valichka, don't listen to him. He's alright, it's just what happened to Mom, he's stressed over that. How are things? How's everything at home?

TOLIK

Yeah, Valichka, how are things in that dorm of yours?

ANTON

Don't listen to him. How is your mom doing?

TOLIK

Look, do you know her?

ANTON

Not at all.

AUNT SHURA

He doesn't.

VALICHKA

He doesn't.

TOLIK

You do. Sure you do. How do you know her, bro?

ANTON

I don't know her. Just wanted to talk.

TOLIK

What are you all hiding here? Like hell you don't know her... I can see the way you've been looking at her all day. How did you get here?

(*He turns to Valichka.*)

You there! Who are you?

AUNT SHURA
Tolya!

TOLIK
Not now, Aunt Shura.

AUNT SHURA
Tolya!

TOLIK
You heard me.

ANTON
Alright now, Tokh', quit it.

TOLIK
Why should I, eh? What are you hiding, you asshole?

Tolik jumps to his feet, and so does Anton. Anton runs to the couch, rips the fur coat off of Mashka, throws it at Tolik, jumps at him and knocks him to the ground. They fight in silence. Kolya steps in, tries to pull Anton off by his leg. Anton fights him, too, while also reaching for Tolik.

TOLIK
You are all in it together! You ganged up! How do you know her? How did they get here?

ANTON
Forgot to ask you!

TOLIK
Asshole.

ANTON
You are!

TOLIK
Go on! Take them and get out of here!

ANTON
Yeah, forgot to ask you!

MASHKA
Kolya!

Everyone stops and looks at Mashka. She is sitting up on the couch, awake, trying to understand what's happening.

MASHKA
What are you doing? Jesssus Christ, Kolya. Did you get any sleep?

KOLYA
(*not letting go of Anton's leg*)
It's alright, Mash', don't worry about anything.

ANTON
Let go my leg.

Kolya releases Anton and goes to Mashka. So does Aunt Shura.

KOLYA
>How are you?

MASHKA
>With all this, I don't feel like having a baby
>around you at all. What's with the fighting?
>What time is it?

AUNT SHURA
>It's morning, Mash', it's morning already. We're
>gonna go.

MASHKA
>Where? Where will you all go?

AUNT SHURA
>To have your baby, Mash'.

(*He turns to everyone.*)

>Pack up. No use sitting here. Go on, pack up.

*Valichka and Katia get up and begin to pick up things
from the floor. Tolik gets up, puts on the fur coat, and
stands wearing it, wavering. The men turn off the cell
phone flashlights and put the phones into their pockets.*

IV

We are left a world filled with joy, the world
of our hope, the world of anticipation. It
was our hands that built it, our dreams that
spun it, and it will be the safe haven for us,
our home and shelter, the stronghold we
pass on to our children. We are left with the
voices of those we loved. We are left with the
memory of what we lost. We will brim with
the poignancy of memory, the power of our
experience, the miracle of our shared universe.
We will be comforted by the sweetness of what
was said, the depth of what we had heard and
endured, we will be made weak by the sun and
disconsolate by the new moon.

...Still refusing to learn how to live without
you, refusing to accept your absence, refusing
to consent to death, to negotiate with death, or
make peace with it....

*Everyone is gathered around the table. On the
table: bundles, bags, Anton's briefcase. ANTON
is wearing a suit. TOLIK is wearing the fur coat.
Everyone is focused. VALICHKA and KATIA are
holding up MASHKA from both sides.*

AUNT SHURA
(to Mashka)
> We'll take our time. We'll take as long as
> we need.

MASHKA
> Thanks, Aunt Shura. As long as these guys don't
> kill each other.

AUNT SHURA
> They won't. I won't allow it.

MASHKA
> Kolya, you okay? Need something to eat?

KOLYA
> I'm here, right here. Don't worry.

ANTON
> I almost forgot!

Anton goes to the fridge, pulls out the cans of food, and packs them into his briefcase. The others watch him in silence.

AUNT SHURA
> Alright? Let's go.

TOLIK
> Nope.

Tolik takes off the fur coat.

ANTON
Tokh', what now?

TOLIK
Something's fishy.

ANTON
Like what?

TOLIK
No one's shooting out there, right?

ANTON
Thank God.

TOLIK
And the crops been burning for two days straight.

ANTON
Yeah, yeah. Come on, let's go.

TOLIK
And no one's come to fight the fire, right? Even though there's no shooting.

ANTON
Well, the bridge is gone!

TOLIK
Right. Except you all got here somehow, never mind the bridge.

KOLYA

Tokh', what's this about?

TOLIK

Where do you think you are going, Kolya?

KOLYA

Me? To have the baby. What about you, Tokh'? You plan to stay here?

TOLIK

Where exactly are you gonna have this baby? On the beach?

AUNT SHURA

We'll find people. We'll get help.

TOLIK

Aunt Shura, where are you taking them? You know perfectly well there's no help out there.

AUNT SHURA

What do you mean, no help?

TOLIK

Just like that. And you know it. Yet you still want to go. Why is that?

AUNT SHURA

Tolik...

KOLYA
(*interrupts, to Tolik*)
> What's this now? What's this you're starting?
> You wanna sit here? You sit! Until your mom
> turns into a hot dog.

MASHKA
> Kolya! Stop it!

KOLYA
> Why Kolya now? We need to leave.

(*He turns to Anton.*)

> Open the door, come on.

ANTON
> Quit yelling. You've got the keys.

*Kolya takes one step toward the door, then stops and looks
back. Everyone looks anxiously at him. Kolya looks like he
wants to say something, but he stops himself. He produces
the key and opens the door. Now the impulse overcomes
him: he turns around and walks back to the table.*

KOLYA
> You drive me nuts, d'you know that?

TOLIK
> No idea. I thought we got along fine.

KOLYA
> Ass-s-hole.

He turns sharply back to the door and comes face to face with RINAT. Rinat is standing in the door, with a grave face, silent. Everyone looks back at him frightened.

RINAT
What are you guys up to?

AUNT SHURA
You? What are you doing here.

Rinat pushes Kolya out of his way, walks to the table and sits down. Tolik hesitates for a moment, then sits down next to him.

RINAT
(*to Tolik, pointing to the women*)
Who are these?

TOLIK
Fuck if I know.

RINAT
Okay to talk around them?

TOLIK
They are deaf. But they read lips.

Rinat gets up abruptly and takes a seat on the other side of the table, with his back to the women.

RINAT
Where do you think you are all going?

TOLIK

Downtown.

RINAT

I see. Your mom here?

TOLIK

Upstairs.

RINAT

Take her with you?

TOLIK

How?

RINAT

I see.

ANTON

How did you know about Mom?

RINAT

The smell.

(*He turns to Tolik.*)

Basically. You can't go there. The ones who were there are gone, and the other ones came in. They put new flags on the Commandant's office.

ANTON

What do you mean, new flags? Who has the post office, telegraph, and the train stations now?

RINAT

The post office? They burned my post office. To the ground.

ANTON

Yeah, we know. You are a mailman without the mail now.

RINAT

(*to* Anton, *aggressively*)

D'you think that's funny?

ANTON

(*mildly*)

No, not at all.

RINAT

Good.

(*He turns to Tolik.*)

Basically, you should not go there. Do you get me?

TOLIK

I got you.

KOLYA
Mashka's having a baby.

Rinat looks at Mashka.

MASHKA
If Kolya says I am, I guess I am.

RINAT
(to Kolya)
Let her do it here. It's quiet here, nice and quiet, perfect for having babies.

KOLYA
And what are you now, the expert?

RINAT
Why? Are you the one in labor?

KOLYA
(offended)
Just. Don't go telling us what to do.

RINAT
You don't say.

(He turns to Tolik.)

Stay put. Wait it out, then you can see. You got me?

TOLIK
I got you.

ANTON

I didn't. What about Mom?

RINAT

Which part did you not get? Your mom'll have to wait.

ANTON

She won't wait, in this heat.

RINAT

Put her in the fridge.

ANTON

How about I stuff you into that fridge, eh?

RINAT

Go ahead, give it a shot.

He gets to his feet, comes to face Anton. Anton cannot hold his stare and backs down. Rinat goes back to his seat.

TOLIK
(*in a low voice*)

No power. Phones are running out.

ANTON

Tokh', what's wrong with you? Are you like, if we had power, you'd put her in the fridge?

TOLIK
(*to Anton*)

Shut up.

ANTON
Why?

TOLIK
(very quietly)
Shut up.

RINAT
(to Tolik)
Sit it out, Tokh'. You, of all people, should not
show your face downtown.

TOLIK
Got it.

KOLYA
What's new there? What are these new people
saying?

RINAT
They said they'll hang all the farmers.

KOLYA
Why farmers?

RINAT
They said, farmers talk too much.

KOLYA
Oh, come on!

RINAT
Also, farmers are fat.

KOLYA

That's it. I'm not listening.

Kolya goes to the front door, locks it with his key, comes back and takes a seat at the table.

RINAT
(*to the women*)

You sit down, too. There's nowhere for you to go.

Mashka breaks away from the women, goes to the couch, plops down, and starts to cry. Kolya goes to her, tries to comfort her.

KOLYA

Mash', come on. It's okay.

MASHKA

What's okay? It's not okay! Who are you people? Why are you so afraid of each other?

KOLYA

I ain't afraid of no one.

MASHKA

How am I supposed to have a baby with you?

KOLYA
(*stands up sharply*)

You know what, I'd be happy to do it myself! I've had it with you all! Who am I doing this for? What am I, special? We're all stuck here in this trap, with nowhere to go. You think I planned that? I've got my crops burning out there. I don't give a flying fuck about your politics. I've no one to hide from, I did nothing! I see you all keep secrets around here. I've got machinery out there in the field. It's probably gone now. And you, too! Now you have to have this baby?

MASHKA
(*gets up, comforts him*)
Okay, Kolya, okay. I'm sorry.

KOLYA
I know.

MASHKA
Alright now.

(*She hugs him.*)

You got no sleep last night. And no food.

RINAT
That will do him good. I mean, healthwise.

Everyone feels awkward, says nothing, looks away.

TOLIK
(*to Rinat*)
What about our guys?

RINAT
They all ran. As soon as the new ones showed, ours packed up and left.

TOLIK

Left their homes?

RINAT

How else? These new ones, they're going door to door, with lists. Looking for everyone.

TOLIK

Is anyone left?

RINAT

I doubt it. They were looking for you. He was with us, they said, until he ran. They wanted to come here.

TOLIK

Why didn't they?

RINAT

The bridge is gone, remember? But you're on their lists, so these new ones, they'll definitely come. Eventually.

TOLIK

What if they can't find it?

RINAT

Like hell they won't. They've got a list. And there's no one else on this street.

TOLIK

So what now?

RINAT
God knows.

(*He turns to Anton.*)

Where's your car?

ANTON
They'll give it back. I'll sort it out.

RINAT
Right.

ANTON
You think they won't?

RINAT
Who'd you leave it with?

ANTON
I don't know. Whoever was in charge.

RINAT
You can go look for him in Rostov now.

ANTON
Shit.

RINAT
(*to Kolya*)
Hey, what about your car?

KOLYA
I've got it. No gas though.

RINAT
Right. Well, you are fucked.

AUNT SHURA
And where are you planning to go?

RINAT
(*to her*)
What?

AUNT SHURA
Where are you going, I asked. You're not about to stay here with us, are you?

RINAT
Why not?

AUNT SHURA
Well. You've got nowhere to go, don't you?

RINAT
How would you know?

AUNT SHURA
I read your lips.

RINAT
You, Aunt Shura, should not worry your pretty little head about me, okay?

AUNT SHURA
　　Okay, I won't. You worry your own head about.

(*She turns to the women.*)

　　Let's unpack.

The women take the bundles off the table, untie them on the floor, and start sorting through the things inside them. They pay no attention to others.

RINAT
(*to Tolik*)
　　Are they really deaf?

TOLIK
　　Hell if I know.

RINAT
　　Anyway, the Greek. Remember him?

TOLIK
　　So?

RINAT
　　He fucked off with the cash. The whole battalion's wages for two months. Remember Shama?

TOLIK
　　I do.

RINAT
　　He flipped.

TOLIK

How?

RINAT

Just like that. Crossed over to the other side. Told them he was in an affective state before.

TOLIK

For three months?

RINAT

Yep. And remember Rooster? He was elected.

TOLIK

Yeah.

RINAT

Got his head blown off.

TOLIK

Fuck.

RINAT

Valik is gone. So's Hosha. The Cripple. Everyone's mad at you. They think you flipped, too.

TOLIK

I didn't.

RINAT

I know. But the others don't.

TOLIK
>And how are we supposed to get out.

RINAT
>I don't know. Fire's all around. It's the truce.

Anton goes to the fridge, produces several bottles of beer, and puts them on the table.

ANTON
(to Rinat)
>Have some?

RINAT
>No. I'm religious, remember?

ANTON
>So am I.

Opens one and takes a long drink looking the whole time at Rinat. Rinat stares back at him. Finally, Anton can't hold his stare, puts his unfinished beer on the table, and walks away.

KOLYA
>Everyone's fucking religious now.

RINAT
>Is something wrong?

KOLYA

Nothing's wrong. Everything's just right. Someone gives to the church, someone else takes. Only losers tithe.

RINAT

That's in your church. We have a different God. He's got no use for your tithe.

AUNT SHURA
(*as she sorts through the clothes*)

There's only one God. Just different languages.

KOLYA

Oh, come on, Aunt Shura! How do you mean, one? How could he

(*he points to Rinat*)

and I have the same God? He's a fucking Tatar. And I mean it in the best sense possible.

RINAT

You watch out now. Redneck.

KOLYA

I just said it to put things simply.

(*He turns to Aunt Shura.*)

So don't even start.

AUNT SHURA

There's only one God. And only one church.
Rinat just doesn't see it—for the time being.
Eventually he will. He might. Tell me, Rinat, is
the church still there?

RINAT

Yep, it's fine. Locked up. The priest left.

AUNT SHURA

That's alright. As long as the church is there.

RINAT

The church is there. But they burned down the
railway station. And the supermarket. And my
post office. What kind of a mailman am I now?

KOLYA

We'll build back.

RINAT

You'll have to do that without me. I'm not going
back there.

AUNT SHURA

Everything can be built back. That much is true.
The bridge can be repaired, too. Who else is
left there?

RINAT

Someone is. It's only the lot of you that's stuck
here. There—there are people. Authorities.

KOLYA

From where I sit, I don't see this church opening again any time soon.

AUNT SHURA

What are you talking about?

KOLYA

I'm talking about the way things are. After everything that's happened—what church are you talking about? The priest is running around the village with an RPG. There are tanks parked inside the church fence. Fucking religion...

AUNT SHURA

What are you talking about?

KOLYA

I'm talking about how it is. I tithed. Apparently so that they can burn me down now together with my combines. But that's not the point. You think I'm sore about the money? I'm not. I'm about the tanks parked inside the church fence. That seems to be against the rules, ain't it?

RINAT

What rules are you talking about? Everyone's surviving the way they can. There's just too much death around us. There aren't enough rules for that. Or words.

AUNT SHURA

Words indeed. We ran out of those first.
Everything broke down, everyone talks their
own way, no one's listening to anyone. No one
understands anyone. Just like us here. Look at
how we're talking.

KOLYA

Seems alright to me.

AUNT SHURA

Right? People can understand you when you
speak right. Do you get it?

KOLYA

I do.

AUNT SHURA

And who understands you, Kolya? No one. No
one can hear you. And no one understands.

RINAT

That's the truth. What's the church got to do
with it?

AUNT SHURA

Nothing. All of this will end, eventually. Life will
go on. Everyone has to go on living somehow—
those who ran and those who didn't, both. They
must live. People will have to come back here.
You can't just sit everything out on this side of
the river. They'll put the bridge back, everything
will come alive again.

ANTON

Come alive how? Where? Not everything, Aunt Shura. Our mom won't come alive again.

AUNT SHURA

You know what I'd like to tell you? About your mom. I remember well what happened back then. With Anna. She was like a daughter to your mom. It was summer, too... And then that grief...

ANTON

Aunt Shura...

AUNT SHURA

Yes, it was summer. Your mom was like she had died. Never left the house. I came to visit every night. Just to sit and visit. We talked. Actually, I talked, and she sat there. And then it was almost the end of summer, there were so many apples. I came one day, and there she was, fussing around the house, sorting things. "Hello," she says to me. As if nothing happened. As if she didn't just spend two months without a word. "Hi," I reply, "everything alright?" "It's fine," she says. "Only Tolik's having a tough time." She talked to me about you, Tolya, how things were for you. She kept me with her a long time that day.

ANTON

Yeah, and then it was fall.

AUNT SHURA

I remember well, the way she came around then—like she'd been frozen still and was slowly warming. She found things to do, things to take care of. Even the way she sounded was different—calmer. One day, we will all sound different again. Calmer. Some day later.

KOLYA

Unless it all burns down first.

AUNT SHURA

Let it burn. Maybe it's meant to be. Let's go. What are we doing sitting here? Don't be afraid. As long as there's somewhere to go, we need to go.

KOLYA

That's right. We need to go.

ANTON

We do. Probably.

AUNT SHURA

Masha, how are you? Can you go?

MASHKA
(*getting to her feet*)
Well, it's not like I can quit on this one

(*she points to Kolya*),

is it? Much as I'd like to.

AUNT SHURA
    That's my girl.

ANTON
    Let me just go check on Mom.

Anton climbs the stairs.

VALICHKA
(*to Anton*)
    Tosha, wait, we'll come with you. Then we'll get
    home together.

She and Katia climb the stairs after Anton. After a while, all come back down.

ANTON
(*to Tolik*)
    Bro, you want to put some clothes back on?

Tolik goes to the wardrobe and stands there in a tense silence.

KOLYA
    Go ahead, open. Get whatever you've got there.

AUNT SHURA
    Open it, Tolya.

MASHKA
    Go on, Tol'.

Tolik turns, leans against the wardrobe, and looks at everyone else for a long moment. Finally, he opens the wardrobe and pulls out the photo album that he and Anton had looked through earlier. He brings it to the table, opens it flat. Everyone gathers around him.

TOLIK
(*to Rinat*)
> How many were we? In our class?

RINAT
> Why are you asking?

TOLIK
> Come on, how many?

RINAT
> Twenty-seven.

TOLIK
> How many girls?

RINAT
> Fifteen.

TOLIK
> That's right. And twelve boys.

ANTON
> Like the apostles.

TOLIK
(*to Anton*)
   Shut up. Twelve. Like the apostles. Look.

Tolik turns the pages of the album until he finds the one he wants.

TOLIK
   Look, it's just the boys here.

RINAT
   Right. There's me.

TOLIK
   Right. Twelve guys. Right?

ANTON
   Right.

TOLIK
   Shut up. Here's Hena.

KOLYA
   Yep.

TOLIK
   Someone stabbed him to death on the train. In his sleeping compartment. Back in May when it all was just starting. Got put on the train alive one night and gotten off dead the next morning.

RINAT
   Any chance he got on the train dead?

TOLIK

Possibly. I wasn't there. He was the first one. Next, Denys. See him here? With his goalie gloves. They beat him to death in the park.

RINAT

Yeah, I know.

TOLIK

Do you know who did it?

RINAT

I don't.

TOLIK

I think you do.

RINAT

How would I?

TOLIK

Everyone knows. Our own guys did it.

RINAT

How do you know?

TOLIK

Everyone knows. Right, Valichka?

Valichka, nervous, steps away from the table. Kolya goes after her, saying soothing things.

MASHKA

Kolya, I don't want to listen to this.

KOLYA

Not now, Mash'.

TOLIK

Exactly. Here's Svyat. He was the shortest, right?

RINAT

Right.

KOLYA

I know him, too.

TOLIK

He hanged himself. D'you know that?

RINAT

I do.

TOLIK

Do you know why?

RINAT

Why?

TOLIK

They said it ran in the family. His dad hanged himself too. And his brother died in a car crash.

RINAT

Shit.

TOLIK
Remember Slavik?

RINAT
Sure. I can see where you're going with this.
Slavik disappeared. With someone else's woman.
I know.

TOLIK
So do I. Can you find Syova?

Rinat studies the picture carefully.

RINAT
There he is. In the middle. He had TB, the open
form. I remember him. He was at a checkpoint,
stopped to show his paper, and it got shelled.
A few weeks ago.

ANTON
Exactly.

RINAT
And there's Friedman.

KOLYA
The Jew.

RINAT
Yes. They ran him out of town.

TOLIK
Killed him.

RINAT
Ran him out of town.

TOLIK
Ran him out of town and then killed him.

RINAT
Right.

Everyone is silent, looking at the picture.

AUNT SHURA
What about the others?

TOLIK
The others? The others went to fight.

AUNT SHURA
And where are they now?

TOLIK
(*to Rinat*)
Where are they?

RINAT
Well, you know... The Greek is gone.
With the money.

KOLYA
Shit.

RINAT
My feelings exactly.

TOLIK

What about the Screech?

RINAT

Heard they saw him in Russia.

TOLIK

What's up with him?

RINAT

He fucked off.

ANTON

Ha! Good choice.

AUNT SHURA

Shut up.

RINAT

Valik's gone too.

TOLIK

Gone?

RINAT

Gone. His post was on the bridge. To the end.
The Cripple is gone too.

TOLIK

Gone?

RINAT

Gone. He was a professor, too.

ANTON

Wasn't he too young to be a professor?

RINAT

Why not? He was thirty—just about right. Was.
I'm the only one left alive. From our whole class.

AUNT SHURA

No, you're not. There should be another one.
The twelfth boy. The last one.

*Everyone starts to count boys in the photo, trying to
figure it out.*

TOLIK

I'm the twelfth. I am the last one.

AUNT SHURA

You?

TOLIK

Sure me. I was always the last one. I was a year
young, remember? They added me to this class
after we moved here. So yeah, I am the last one.

ANTON

That's some class you've got there... Then
again—mine's the same.

KOLYA

We had quite the school.

AUNT SHURA

You had a regular, normal school. It was the times that did it.

ANTON

I don't know about the times. Seems regular to me. We all grew up, didn't we? Found jobs.

KOLYA

You mean, work.

AUNT SHURA

Those were miserable times. And so are these. So don't blame your school.

TOLIK

I suppose you're the one to know. You used to work there.

AUNT SHURA

I did. A long time ago.

Everyone is silent, studying the picture.

TOLIK

So, the Greek is gone, right?

RINAT

Yeah.

TOLIK

And the Screech?

RINAT
The Screech, too.

TOLIK
And Valik. And the Cripple.

RINAT
Don't be scared. None of our guys are left.

TOLIK
I'm not scared of our people. Or the other people. I'm scared of myself.

ANTON
Oh, don't start.

TOLIK
I'm not starting anything. The dead don't scare me. Easier to get along with them these days than with the living.

RINAT
Boy, you said it. The dead don't breathe down your neck.

MASHKA
Kol', I want to go home.

KOLYA
So do I, Mash'. So do I.

RINAT
The dead don't turn their people in. Aunt Shura?

AUNT SHURA
What?

RINAT
Tell me, how can you turn in your own people?

AUNT SHURA
Your own?

RINAT
Uh-huh. Over the phone. How can someone do
that? Just call the other side and say, here, I've
got one of the guys you want, here's his number,
address, come get him. How is that possible?
Politics, different views, electoral moods—I get
all that. But to turn your own people in? Tell me!
I don't remember being taught that in school.

AUNT SHURA
You know, Rinat, there were many things you
weren't taught in that school. Such as blowing
up bridges. Or setting the crops on fire. And
you do.

RINAT
Who? Me?

AUNT SHURA
You, who else.

RINAT
Me?

TOLIK

You. Us... It was us, wasn't it?

RINAT

Are you nuts?

TOLIK

Don't think so. You know it. We all know everything. We're just not going to say a word. What's there to say? Where am I supposed to go? Do you think, if there's a truce that means everything's over? Do you think they'll just build the bridge back, and that's it? Who's going to use it? Where are people supposed to go. A truce... Maybe you have a truce. I'm not about to make peace with anyone. For me, this war started a while ago. Back when I lost Anya. Been fighting ever since.

AUNT SHURA

Against whom?

TOLIK

Everyone.

AUNT SHURA

And how's it going?

TOLIK

Could be better. And Mom is now gone, too. You, brother, you keep saying family this, family that. Do you know I did her laundry there, at the end? She didn't want to touch it. I fed her, too. When I was home, I mean. There's a war on, we're all fighting. And now Mom is gone. Everyone's gone. And there's nowhere to go.

RINAT
Alright. I'll tell them at the headquarters.

TOLIK
You do that. They pay you money for it.

RINAT
Yeah, I'm rolling in it.

(*He turns to everyone.*)

So, what? Shall we? I'll come with you, I don't want to stay here. With this one. He's nuts.

KOLYA
You aren't afraid to come with?

RINAT
Ah, what's the difference now? They're people still, right?

KOLYA
Then why did you come here.

RINAT
Wanted to see this one.

(*He points to Tolik.*)

KOLYA

And now you have.

RINAT

I have. I'd been better off if I didn't.

KOLYA

Then we should go. Tokh', are you sure?

TOLIK

You go ahead. While it's cool. It'll be harder for Mashka later.

ANTON

What about you, Tokh'? It's not like I can just leave you here.

TOLIK

You can. You've got your carcasses going bad, and I've got Mom.

ANTON

Tokha, don't start again!

TOLIK

Okay, alright, I'm sorry. I'll just wait. When you get there, send someone back here.

ANTON

Alright, Tokh'. Don't worry. I'll sort it all out. I really need to go. Please understand.

TOLIK
I understand.

RINAT
You'll burn here before nightfall. The fire's coming this way.

TOLIK
Nah, I won't. Don't worry.

VALICHKA
He's right, Tokh'. We should go.

MASHKA
Right, Aunt Shura, let's get going. I'm sorry, Tolik.

Aunt Shura approaches Tolik.

AUNT SHURA
You won't come?

TOLIK
Go without me. You know where.

AUNT SHURA
Alright. Everything will be fine.

Anton runs up to Tolik, tries to drag him by his hand.

ANTON
What's wrong with you? Are you nuts, bro? You'll burn here. With her. Let's go now. Come on! Tokh'!

Tolik breaks free and goes to the wardrobe.

TOLIK
> Everything will be fine, brother. You go. You all go, what are you waiting for.

RINAT
> What about you?

TOLIK
> You'll send someone for me.

ANTON
> Who are we gonna send? There's no one there either! Are you nuts? I'd stay with you, but what's the use? Come on, I have to get my car. I've got the meat to take care of. Let's go now, you can come back later. You think I want to leave her like this?

TOLIK
> I don't.

ANTON
> I'll come back, Tokh'. I'll sort it all out and come back.

TOLIK
> Sure. You will sort it all out. You go now.

ANTON
> Okay. I'll get it done. Whatever. I'll sort it out.

(He turns to everyone.)

Let's go.

Anton opens the door and steps outside. Everyone is still standing, silent, wavering.

MASHKA
Kolya...

KOLYA
Yes, Mash'?

MASHKA
Are we going?

Kolya says nothing.

KOLYA
(to Tolik)
Tokh'?

Tolik does not respond.

KOLYA
(to Mashka)
Let's go.

He takes her by the hand and leads her outside.

RINAT
(to Valichka)
Valya? Katia?

VALICHKA
Yes.

RINAT
We should go.

One after the other, the three of them leave.

Aunt Shura lingers, wants to say something to Tolik but does not. She goes to the table, looks at the picture, then closes the album. She leaves. She does not close the door behind her.

Tolik stands in the middle of the room for a while. Then he starts picking things up. He lifts clothes off the floor and tosses them onto the couch. He piles the empty beer bottles in the sink. Puts the chairs upside down on the table. Unrolls the rug.

TOLIK
Fire's everywhere. No matter where you go—it'll get you.

He goes to the wardrobe, opens it, throws the fur coat inside, closes the wardrobe. Has another idea, opens the wardrobe again and pulls out his sniper rifle. Slowly, he climbs to the second floor and goes into his mother's room. He leaves the door open.

A pause.

Steps are heard outside.

Anton enters. He looks around the room and, finding no Tolik, anxiously climbs upstairs, to the bedroom. Mashka and Kolya enter. Mashka is half-whispering, half-sobbing something into Kolya's ear; Kolya tries to comfort her and steers her by her shoulders. They,

*too, slowly climb the stairs and go to the room with the
deceased.*

*Rinat enters. He crosses the room, stops. He goes to
the wardrobe, rips the door open, looks inside, then closes
the door. He climbs the stairs and disappears into the
bedroom.*

*Valichka and Katya enter, conversing in low voices.
They quickly follow the others upstairs.*

*Aunt Shura is the last one to enter. She makes sure
to close and lock the front door. Slowly, she climbs
the stairs. She enters the bedroom and shuts the door
behind her.*

THE END

Recent Titles in the Series
Harvard Library of Ukrainian Literature

Forest Song:
A Fairy Play in Three Acts

Lesia Ukrainka (Larysa Kosach)

Translated by Virlana Tkacz and Wanda Phipps
Introduced by George G. Grabowicz

This play represents the crowning achievement of Lesia Ukrainka's (Larysa Kosach's) mature period and is a uniquely powerful poetic text. Here, the author presents a symbolist meditation on the interaction of mankind and nature set in a world of primal forces and pure feelings as seen through childhood memories and the re-creation of local Volhynian folklore.

2024 | appr. 240 pp.

ISBN 9780674291874 (cloth)	$29.95
9780674291881 (paperback)	$19.95
9780674291898 (epub)	
9780674291904 (PDF)	

Harvard Library of Ukrainian Literature, vol. 13

Read the book online

Love Life: A Novel

Oksana Lutsyshyna

Translated by Nina Murray
Introduced by Marko Pavlyshyn

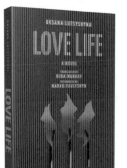

The second novel of the award-winning Ukrainian writer and poet Oksana Lutsyshyna writes the story of Yora, an immigrant to the United States from Ukraine. A delicate soul that's finely attuned to the nuances of human relations, Yora becomes enmeshed in a relationship with Sebastian, a seductive acquaintance who seems to be suggesting that they share a deep bond. After a period of despair and complex grief that follows the end of the relationship, Yora is able to emerge stronger, in part thanks to the support from a friendly neighbor who has adapted well to life on the margins of society.

2024 | 276 pp.

ISBN 9780674297159 (cloth)	$39.95
9780674297166 (paperback)	$19.95
9780674297173 (epub)	
9780674297180 (PDF)	

Harvard Library of Ukrainian Literature, vol. 12

Read the book online

Cecil the Lion Had to Die: A Novel

Olena Stiazhkina

Translated by Dominique Hoffman

This novel follows the fate of four families as the world around them undergoes radical transformations when the Soviet Union unexpectedly implodes, independent Ukraine emerges, and neoimperial Russia begins its war by occupying Ukraine's Crimea and parts of the Donbas. A tour de force of stylistic registers and intertwining stories, ironic voices and sincere discoveries, this novel is a must-read for those who seek to deeper understand Ukrainians from the Donbas, and how history and local identity have shaped the current war with Russia.

2024 | 248 pp.

ISBN 9780674291645 (cloth)	$39.95
9780674291669 (paperback)	$19.95
9780674291676 (epub)	
9780674291683 (PDF)	

Harvard Library of Ukrainian Literature, vol. 11

Read the book online

The City: A Novel

Valerian Pidmohylnyi

Translated with an introduction by Maxim Tarnawsky

This novel was a landmark event in the history of Ukrainian literature. Written by a master craftsman in full control of the texture, rhythm, and tone of the text, the novel tells the story of Stepan, a young man from the provinces who moves to the capital of Ukraine, Kyiv, and achieves success as a writer through a succession of romantic encounters with women.

2024 | 496 pp.

ISBN 9780674291119 (cloth)	$39.95
9780674291126 (paperback)	$19.95
9780674291133 (epub)	
9780674291140 (PDF)	

Harvard Library of Ukrainian Literature, vol. 10

Read the book online

Cassandra:
A Dramatic Poem,

Lesia Ukrainka (Larysa Kosach)

Translated by Nina Murray, introduction by Marko Pavlyshyn

The classic myth of Cassandra turns into much more in Lesia Ukrainka's rendering: Cassandra's prophecies are uttered in highly poetic language—fitting to the genre of the dramatic poem that Ukrainka crafts for this work—and are not believed for that very reason, rather than because of Apollo's curse. Cassandra's being a poet and a woman are therefore the two focal points of the drama.

2024 | 263 pp, bilingual ed. (Ukrainian, English)

ISBN 9780674291775 (hardcover) | $29.95
9780674291782 (paperback) | $19.95
9780674291799 (epub)
9780674291805 (PDF)

Harvard Library of Ukrainian Literature, vol. 8

Read
the book
online

Ukraine, War, Love:
A Donetsk Diary

Olena Stiazhkina

Translated by Anne O. Fisher

In this war-time diary, Olena Stiazhkina depicts day-to-day developments in and around her beloved hometown during Russia's 2014 invasion and occupation of the Ukrainian city of Donetsk.

Summer 2023

ISBN 9780674291690 (hardcover) | $39.95
9780674291706 (paperback) | $19.95
9780674291713 (epub)
9780674291768 (PDF)

Harvard Library of Ukrainian Literature, vol. 7

Read
the book
online

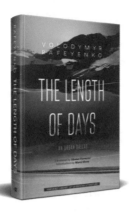

The Length of Days: An Urban Ballad

Volodymyr Rafeyenko

Translated by Sibelan Forrester
Afterword and interview with the author by Marci Shore

This novel is set mostly in the composite Donbas city of Z—an uncanny foretelling of what this letter has come to symbolize since February 24, 2022, when Russia launched a full-scale invasion of Ukraine. Several embedded narratives attributed to an alcoholic chemist-turned-massage therapist give insight into the funny, ironic, or tragic lives of people who remained in the occupied Donbas after Russia's initial aggression in 2014.

2023	349 pp.	
ISBN 780674291201 (cloth)	$39.95
9780674291218 (paper)	$19.95
9780674291225 (epub)	
9780674291232 (PDF)	

Harvard Library of Ukrainian Literature, vol. 6

Read the book online

The Torture Camp on Paradise Street

Stanislav Aseyev

Translated by Zenia Tompkins and Nina Murray

Ukrainian journalist and writer Stanislav Aseyev details his experience as a prisoner from 2015 to 2017 in a modern-day concentration camp overseen by the Federal Security Bureau of the Russian Federation (FSB) in the Russian-controlled city of Donetsk. This memoir recounts an endless ordeal of psychological and physical abuse, including torture and rape, inflicted upon the author and his fellow inmates over the course of nearly three years of illegal incarceration spent largely in the prison called Izoliatsiia (Isolation).

2023	300 pp., 1 map, 18 ill.	
ISBN 9780674291072 (cloth)	$39.95
9780674291089 (paper)	$19.95
9780674291102 (epub)	
9780674291096 (PDF)	

Harvard Library of Ukrainian Literature, vol. 5

Read the book online

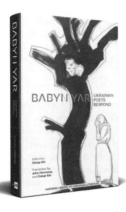

Babyn Yar: Ukrainian Poets Respond

Edited with introduction by Ostap Kin

Translated by John Hennessy and Ostap Kin

In 2021, the world commemorated the 80th anniversary of the massacres of Jews at Babyn Yar. The present collection brings together for the first time the responses to the tragic events of September 1941 by Ukrainian Jewish and non-Jewish poets of the Soviet and post-Soviet periods, presented here in the original and in English translation by Ostap Kin and John Hennessy.

2022	282 pp.	
ISBN 9780674275591 (hardcover)	$39.95	
9780674271692 (paperback)	$16.00	
9780674271722 (epub)		
9780674271739 (PDF)		

Harvard Library of Ukrainian Literature, vol. 4

Read the book online

The Voices of Babyn Yar

Marianna Kiyanovska

Translated by Oksana Maksymchuk and Max Rosochinsky
Introduced by Polina Barskova

With this collection of stirring poems, the award-winning Ukrainian poet honors the victims of the Holocaust by writing their stories of horror, death, and survival in their own imagined voices.

2022	192 pp.	
ISBN 9780674268760 (hardcover)	$39.95	
9780674268869 (paperback)	$16.00	
9780674268876 (epub)		
9780674268883 (PDF)		

Harvard Library of Ukrainian Literature, vol. 3

Read the book online

Mondegreen: Songs about Death and Love

Volodymyr Rafeyenko

Translated and introduced by Mark Andryczyk

Volodymyr Rafeyenko's novel Mondegreen: Songs about Death and Love explores the ways that memory and language construct our identity, and how we hold on to it no matter what. The novel tells the story of Haba Habinsky, a refugee from Ukraine's Donbas region, who has escaped to the capital city of Kyiv at the onset of the Ukrainian-Russian war.

2022	204 pp.	
ISBN 9780674275577 (hardcover)		$39.95
9780674271708 (paperback)		$19.95
9780674271746 (epub)		
9780674271760 (PDF)		

Harvard Library of Ukrainian Literature, vol. 2

Read
the book
online

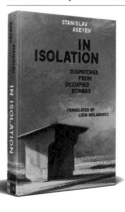

In Isolation: Dispatches from Occupied Donbas

Stanislav Aseyev

Translated by Lidia Wolanskyj

In this exceptional collection of dispatches from occupied Donbas, writer and journalist Stanislav Aseyev details the internal and external changes observed in the cities of Makiïvka and Donetsk in eastern Ukraine.

2022	320 pp., 42 photos, 2 maps	
ISBN 9780674268784 (hardcover)		$39.95
9780674268791 (paperback)		$19.95
9780674268814 (epub)		
9780674268807 (PDF)		

Harvard Library of Ukrainian Literature, vol. 1

Read
the book
online

Recent Titles in the Harvard Series in Ukrainian Studies

The Frontline: Essays on Ukraine's Past and Present

Serhii Plokhy

The Frontline presents a selection of essays drawn together for the first time to form a companion volume to Serhii Plokhy's *The Gates of Europe* and *Chernobyl*. Here he expands upon his analysis in earlier works of key events in Ukrainian history, including Ukraine's complex relations with Russia and the West, the burden of tragedies such as the Holodomor and World War II, the impact of the Chernobyl nuclear disaster, and Ukraine's contribution to the collapse of the Soviet Union.

2021 (HC) / 2023 (PB) | 416 pp. / 420 pp.

10 color photos, 9 color maps

ISBN 9780674268821 (hardcover)	$64.00
9780674268838 (paperback)	$19.95
9780674268845 (epub)	
9780674268852 (PDF)	

Read all chapters online

Harvard Series in Ukrainian Studies, vol. 81

The Moscow Factor: US Policy toward Sovereign Ukraine and the Kremlin

Eugene M. Fishel

Russia's war on Ukraine did not start on February 24, 2022 with the full-scale invasion. Over eight years ago, in 2014, Russia illegally annexed Crimea from Ukraine, fanned a separatist conflict in the Donbas region, and attacked Ukraine with units of its regular army and special forces. In each instance of Russian aggression, the U.S. response has often been criticized as inadequate, insufficient, or hesitant.

2022 | 324 pp., 2 photos

ISBN 9780674279179 (hardcover)	$59.95
9780674279186 (paperback)	$29.95
9780674279421 (epub)	
9780674279193 (PDF)	

Read all chapters online

Harvard Series in Ukrainian Studies, vol. 82

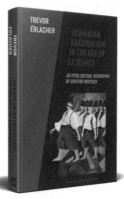

Ukrainian Nationalism in the Age of Extremes: An Intellectual Biography of Dmytro Dontsov

Trevor Erlacher

Ukrainian nationalism made worldwide news after the Euromaidan revolution and the outbreak of the Russo-Ukrainian war in 2014. Invoked by regional actors and international commentators, the "integral" Ukrainian nationalism of the 1930s has moved to the center of debates about Eastern Europe, but the history of this divisive ideology remains poorly understood.

2021 | 658 pp., 34 photos, 5 illustr.

ISBN 9780674250932 (hardcover) | $84.00
9780674250949 (epub)
9780674250956 (Kindle)
9780674250963 (PDF)

Harvard Series in Ukrainian Studies, vol. 80

Read
all chapters
online

Survival as Victory: Ukrainian Women in the Gulag

Oksana Kis

Translated by Lidia Wolanskyj

Hundreds of thousands of Ukrainian women were sentenced to the GULAG in the 1940s and 1950s. Only about half of them survived. With this book, Oksana Kis has produced the first anthropological study of daily life in the Soviet forced labor camps as experienced by Ukrainian women prisoners.
Based on the written memoirs, autobiographies, and oral histories of over 150 survivors, this book fills a lacuna in the scholarship regarding Ukrainian experience.

2020 | 652 pp., 78 color photos, 10 b/w photos

ISBN 9780674258280 (hardcover) | $94.00
9780674258327 (epub)
9780674258334 (Kindle)
9780674258341 (PDF)

Harvard Series in Ukrainian Studies, vol. 79

Read
all chapters
online